PUFFIN BOOKS

Anthony McGowan is a multi-award-winning author of books for adults, teenagers and younger children. He has a life-long obsession with the natural world, and has travelled widely to study and observe it.

D0994947

Books by Anthony McGowan

LEOPARD ADVENTURE

SHARK ADVENTURE

BEAR ADVENTURE

ANTHONY McGOWAN

Illustrated by Nelson Evergreen

PUFFIN

PUFFIN BOOKS

Published by the Penguin Group
Penguin Books Ltd, 80 Strand, London WC2R ORL, England
Penguin Group (USA) Inc., 375 Hudson Street, New York, New York 10014, USA
Penguin Group (Canada), 90 Eglinton Avenue East, Suite 700, Toronto, Ontario, Canada M4P 2Y3
(a division of Pearson Penguin Canada Inc.)
Penguin Ireland, 25 St Stephen's Green, Dublin 2, Ireland (a division of Penguin Books Ltd)
Penguin Group (Australia), 707 Collins Street, Melbourne, Victoria 3008, Australia
(a division of Pearson Australia Group Pty Ltd)
Penguin Books India Pvt Ltd, 11 Community Centre, Panchsheel Park, New Delhi – 110 017, India
Penguin Group (NZ), 67 Apollo Drive, Rosedale, Auckland 0632, New Zealand
(a division of Pearson New Zealand Ltd)
Penguin Books (South Africa) (Pty) Ltd, Block D, Rosebank Office Park,
181 Jan Smuts Avenue, Parktown North, Gauteng 2193, South Africa

Penguin Books Ltd, Registered Offices: 80 Strand, London WC2R ORL, England

puffinbooks.com

First published 2013
001

Text and illustrations copyright © Willard Price Literary Management Ltd, 2013
Map copyright © Puffin Books, 2013
Illustrations by Nelson Evergreen
All rights reserved

The moral right of the author and illustrator has been asserted

Set in 13/16pt Baskerville MT Std
Typeset by Jouve (UK), Milton Keynes
Printed in Great Britain by Clays Ltd, St Ives plc

British Library Cataloguing in Publication Data
A CIP catalogue record for this book is available from the British Library

ISBN: 978-0-141-33951-1

www.greenpenguin.co.uk

ALWAYS LEARNING   **PEARSON**

To my Canadian cousin,
Big John McGowan, 1961–2009

Acknowledgements

My thanks to the whole brilliant Puffin team, especially Anthea Townsend and Samantha Mackintosh. Also to Corinne Turner for keeping the Willard Price flame burning. But most of all my gratitude and admiration goes to Nelson Evergreen for his wonderful illustrations, which bring my words into such spectacular life.

Contents

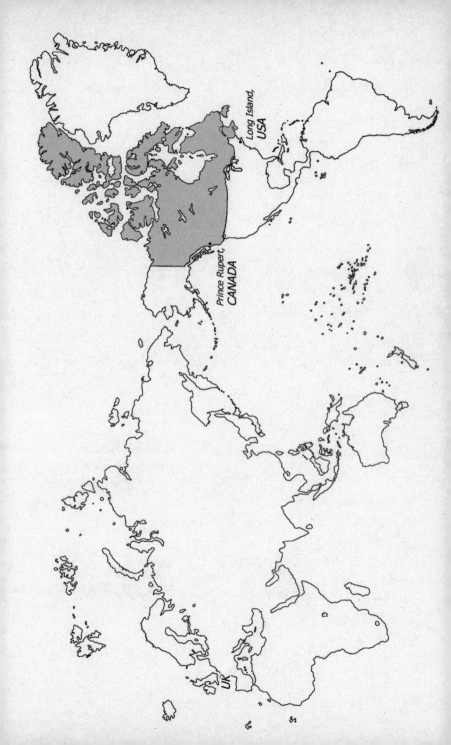

Prelude

He had been travelling south now for a long time. Winters had come and gone, each one a little shorter, a little less cold than the last. He had starved, and he had fed. Early on, the rotting carcass of a grey whale, beached on the shingle, had kept him alive for months. But now that he was grown, there was nothing that he could catch that he could not kill.

Back in the north he had been safe for as long as his mother was alive.

But his mother had fallen down when the tall, thin animals had come with the sticks that made a sound like thunder. A red eye had opened in his mother's chest, and before she died she bit him to make him run away.

And he did run, back to the den that was no longer warm. And then the others came, the white ones, and drove him away. Had he not fled, they would have killed him for being like them and not like them at the same time.

But now he was big. Bigger than the white ones. Bigger even than the biggest of the brown ones through whose territory he now wandered. They feared him, and their fear fed him, like the whale had fed him, filling him with almost as much poison as nourishment.

And now that another year was drawing to its close he was filled with urgency. He had to be fat to get through the winter. He had to eat. His colour was wrong for this place where everything was brown and green – although, now that the leaves were turning, he had begun to blend in, his gold matching theirs. The week before he had killed a moose, a huge creature, taller than a horse. But again he hungered.

And now, as he moved through the forest, he caught a new scent. It was something he had experienced only once before. It was the smell of the animals with the sticks that made thunder. It filled him with excitement and rage and, for the first time in a long while, fear.

But the fear did not cancel out the excitement or the rage. For he knew that, whatever else it might mean, the smell was food.

The Glutton

Fourteen-year-old Frazer Hunt was staring into the eyes of what was, weight for weight, just about the most powerful carnivore in the world. It looked like a stumpy brown bear, but with a longer tail, a smaller head, and with an air of menace that not even a grizzly with a toothache could match. The beast, hunched and forceful, had come trotting along the trail with something in its mouth. It took Frazer a moment or two to work out what it was – at first he'd assumed it was a strangely shaped stick.

But then he realized that this wasn't some friendly, stick-carrying mutt, and that the thing in its mouth was a leg.

A wolf's leg.

Whether the creature had killed the wolf, or simply stumbled across the carcass and torn off this trophy to carry back to its lair, Frazer couldn't say.

It didn't much matter.

The animal stopped in its tracks, raised its broad

snout and sniffed, the sound clear in the cold morning air. Frazer remembered that it had poor eyesight, and depended on a keen sense of smell and hearing to track its prey.

He probably knew more about wild animals than any other fourteen-year-old in the world, but even he'd never seen one of these before. Of course the wilderness was full of shy creatures, but this animal wasn't so much shy as secretive and cunning.

But even as those thoughts played through his mind he was also transfixed by the primal fear of the prey confronted with the predator.

Frazer had stumbled across the scene as he hiked not far from the campsite he was sharing with his father, Hal Hunt, and his cousin, Amazon. They were up here in the thickly forested mountains of Western Canada to help look for Amazon's parents, Roger and Ling-Mei, whose light aircraft had disappeared in this almost endless wilderness weeks earlier.

Hal Hunt was in charge of TRACKS – an organization devoted to saving endangered animals and threatened environments anywhere on the planet. He had thrown the full weight of TRACKS behind trying to find his brother and his sister-in-law – not least because, after years of animosity, the brothers had finally been reconciled, and Roger had been on his way to deliver a vital piece of information to Hal concerning the very existence of TRACKS.

But that wasn't what Frazer was thinking about right now. His thoughts were torn equally between, *How the heck am I going to get out of this one?* and *This is going to make the greatest photo I've ever taken.*

Yep, Frazer had his trusty Leica digital camera with him, and he'd set out that morning planning to snap something. He'd been hoping for a deer, or a bald eagle, but he'd found something much more interesting.

And dangerous.

He ran through what he'd read or heard about the beast: Latin name *Gulo gulo* – meaning the glutton. And it was well named. This glutton would eat anything it could get hold of. And once it had hold of something it wouldn't let go or stop eating until it had consumed every last scrap – meat, skin, even bones.

Its jaws and teeth were perfect for the job – strong enough to crack open a moose's thigh bone to get at the pink marrow within. In fact, it could bite through bone the way Frazer could chew through a candy bar.

Nothing stood up to a full-grown *Gulo gulo* – not wolves, not bears, not even the big cougars that were still common in this part of Canada.

Yes, at last Frazer was confronting the brutal boss of the northern forest, the wolverine.

And now this wolverine was sniffling and snuffling, tasting the air. He – and Frazer was pretty sure that it was a he – knew Frazer was somewhere close, and he was using that sensitive snout of his to home in.

Frazer half wished that he'd brought the X-Ark – the world's best tranq rifle. TRACKS used a special knock-out drug in the darts that could put down a grizzly in three seconds. But all Frazer had was his camera, and he doubted that the wolverine would be vain enough to stop its charge and pose for a picture.

Frazer stood perfectly still. He thought over his options. He could climb a tree, or he could run for his life, hoping to reach camp before the loping predator caught up with him.

He'd once heard tell of a wolverine that had chased a half-grown black bear up a tree. The bear got stuck, and the wolverine spent the next week taking bites out of the poor bear's backside, until the creature finally perished from cold and hunger and loss of blood.

Or maybe just plain embarrassment.

That wasn't how Frazer planned to go.

He began to back away, keeping his eyes firmly on the wolverine. Slowly does it, he said to himself. He fought to control his breathing, keeping it steady. Breath was the secret to so many things, from making a good clean shot with a tranq gun to catching a trout with a fly in a cold mountain stream.

Step by step he moved away from the wolverine, putting each foot down as delicately as if it were made of nitroglycerine.

It was working. The wolverine stopped sniffing at the air, dipped its head once more and turned off the track, still carrying that leg in its powerful mouth.

Frazer began to think about how he'd tell Amazon and his dad about the encounter. He'd say he'd faced the wolverine down, stared back fearlessly into those black eyes until the creature had realized that it had met its match, and turned and run.

So what he needed was a little bit of evidence to prove that he was telling the truth. What he needed was that photo. He even thought that he might be able to sell the picture to a magazine. He'd always wanted to get something in the *National Geographic*, and this would be the ideal opportunity. Not even professional wildlife photographers got many snaps of wily old *Gulo gulo*.

The camera was in its leather case, hanging from a strap round his neck. He carefully lifted the case and, holding his breath, eased it open. He'd been terrified that the sound of the popper unfastening might be loud enough to alert the wolverine, but still the beast trotted on. Now Frazer had to be quick. In another couple of seconds it would disappear into the trees, and he'd never see it again.

He raised the camera to eye level.

He could not stop his hands from trembling ever so slightly, but the camera had built-in stabilization, so that should be fine, as long as he chose a fast enough shutter speed.

He looked through the viewfinder. He had the perfect shot. The wolverine had stopped again, just before the treeline. Its front paws were on a small boulder and, in the distance, mountains loomed up, their sharp, snow-tipped peaks echoing the teeth of the wolverine. It was staring right at the camera lens, that gruesome leg balanced in its mouth.

This was perfect. It was going to make Frazer famous.

He clicked.

And as he clicked he realized what he had done. The wolverine was looking up because it had caught a whiff of him. Its teeth were bared because it was offering a threat to the unseen challenger for this meal of wolf leg.

And now with the click of the shutter – and it really was such a very tiny noise – the wolverine had gone from yellow to red alert. Now it had something solid to go on, it zeroed in on Frazer, sniffing deeply.

It had him.

Now even the weak eyes were focused.

It spat out the bony leg and began to make its cry.

Frazer had heard the roar of a male lion as it stalked him in the African bush; he had heard the higher-pitched snarl of a man-eating leopard; he had heard the deadly hiss of a spitting cobra, aiming its spray of venom at his eyes; he had heard the snarl of a leaping jaguar and the splash from the tail of a tiger shark beginning its killer-surge; but this stream

8

of yelps, yaps, yips, growls and snickering was the most terrifying sound he had ever come across.

And that was it. Frazer's coolness, his hard-earned calm under pressure, fled and he followed. He turned and he ran.

It was like running away from a monster in a dream. His legs wouldn't seem to move properly.

The thick leaf mould on the ground sucked at his legs, pulling him down. He could hear the quick scampering feet of the wolverine behind him. He imagined its jaws sinking into the seat of his pants. That gave him another spurt of panic-fuelled energy. He escaped from the soft leaf mould and found the firmer ground of the trail he had been following. The pine and larch trees closed over him, but now he was moving more quickly, his long legs eating up the ground.

He glanced over his shoulder, thinking that the wolverine might have given up on him and gone back to the dead wolf, which was, at least, a meal that had stopped trying to escape.

What he saw almost made him scream. The wolverine was only about two metres away. Its strange loping gait – with each limb seeming to go off in a different direction – was almost comical. But there was nothing funny at all in the look of deadly intent on that vicious face. In fact, all that stopped Frazer from screaming was the shame he would feel if his cousin and father heard him. The Hunts were not a screaming family. They were the sort of people who faced whatever the world threw at them with a grim smile. Screaming wasn't an option.

Then he saw the flash of colour ahead of him. It was the orange of the tent he shared with Amazon. His heart leapt with hope. On he raced. He jumped over a tree trunk that had fallen across the trail.

Again he glanced back, hoping that the obstacle might have deterred the wolverine. But no, it somehow managed to squirm under the log. But squirming is a lot slower than running, and Frazer gained a few vital seconds.

Four more metres and he was there, right in the middle of the campsite, shouting out at the top of his voice. His father was by the fire, cleaning his hunting rifle, an ancient bolt-action Lee-Enfield, dating back to the First World War.

'Dad,' screamed Frazer, pointing frantically behind him, 'quick, shoot!'

He didn't, of course, mean 'shoot the wolverine'. He just wanted his father to shoot the gun in the air to scare it off.

Amazon Hunt stuck her head out of the tent to see what all the commotion was about. Her face showed first puzzlement and then, as she saw the danger Frazer was in, horror. Amazon might not have come across many wolverines back in her boarding school in England before she joined TRACKS, but she certainly knew all about the grim reputation of the glutton.

Hal Hunt stood up. In late middle age he was still fit and lean, hard muscle covering his well-knit frame. With his close-cropped grey hair, he exuded a sense of power and competence. Frazer also knew that his dad was a magnificent shot, whether he had a tranq gun, high-powered rifle or slingshot in his strong hands. Yep, he was exactly the kind of person you wanted to see when a deadly predator was on your tail. He'd ping a bullet right under the wolverine's nose to scare it off. And if that didn't work . . . well, he loved his son even more than he loved other animals, right?

But then, with dismay, Frazer saw that his father had left his rifle on the ground. In its place he'd picked up a rock.

What was he doing?

'Yah! Yah!' shouted Hal Hunt, waving his arms in the air.

Frazer looked back at the wolverine. It had stopped on the edge of the campsite. It stood on its stumpy back legs and again made that infernal chattering sound that seemed to combine both an insult and a threat.

Then Hal Hunt threw the rock. It hit the ground in front of the wolverine. The creature started to shy away. But then it stopped, sniffed again at the air and gave a low growl, which, to Frazer, seemed to say, 'I could quite easily eat you all if I felt like it.' After lingering for another moment, to Frazer's utter relief, it slowly turned away in an unhurried fashion and walked into the forest with its nose held high in the air.

Frazer looked over at Amazon, who was making a noise not unlike that made by the wolverine. The look on her face wasn't, it turned out, fear for his safety. It was mirth. His cousin was laughing fit to burst.

Puzzled, Frazer looked back at his father. Hal Hunt had his hand over his mouth, trying to hide a broad smile.

2

The Search Party

'What are you all laughing at?' asked Frazer. 'That thing nearly got me!'

'What, the weasel?' gasped Amazon, in between her guffaws.

'That wasn't a weasel, it was a wolverine. They're famously vicious.'

'The wolverine,' said Hal Hunt calmly, 'is, technically, the world's second biggest member of the mustelids, the weasel family. The first is the giant otter, which you may remember from your trip down the Amazon last year. And yes, the wolverine is pretty feisty, but you really weren't in any danger. Did you disturb it at a kill?'

'Yes,' said Frazer. 'Sort of. It had a wolf's leg in its mouth.'

'It was just protecting its dinner,' Hal continued. 'The wolverine's fearsome reputation has been greatly exaggerated. There's no record of a person ever having been harmed by one. You'd only be in danger if you were weak or trapped in a snowdrift.'

Frazer rolled his eyes at the lecture. He liked to show off his wilderness expertise in front of Amazon, who was a little younger than him. But there's nothing like being told off by your dad to make you feel like a little kid.

The three of them had flown out that morning from the gritty frontier town of Prince Rupert. Hal Hunt piloted the aircraft himself – a tough little de Havilland floatplane laden with the expedition gear, including two mountain bikes strapped to the outside of the fuselage. The plane had struggled to get over the white peaks and high ice fields of the Canadian Coast Mountains. During her recent adventures in Russia and Polynesia, Amazon had seen many astounding sights, with crags reaching into the heavens and valleys cutting into the earth below, but these mountains were a match for any of them. They also held a new threat: the promise of the winter to come.

They had landed on the perfectly flat waters of a small tear-shaped lake, glistening like mercury in the autumn sunshine. Circling over the lake before landing, they had seen nothing but forest, mountains and more lakes. Not the remotest sign that human beings had ever set foot in this beautiful wilderness.

'You'd never guess,' said Hal Hunt, crackling over the intercom, 'that this is one of the oldest inhabited parts of North America. Fourteen thousand years ago the earliest Americans walked over from Siberia to Alaska, and moved down the western coast. Within a thousand years, they reached the very bottom of South America.'

'Walked?' Amazon had asked. 'Isn't there a sea in between Alaska and Siberia?'

'Correct – the Bering Strait – but back then the world was in the grip of the last ice age. So much of the sea was locked up in the ice that a land bridge was left exposed, and those good old Siberians just walked right across.'

But they weren't here in this remote corner of Canada to go sightseeing. Nor were they here on a conservation mission. They were here to find Amazon's parents, Roger and Ling-Mei Hunt, whose own light aircraft had gone missing somewhere in this wilderness.

The authorities had given up on the search: there were so many thousands of square miles of virgin forest . . . And, as the police had pointed out, the time that had elapsed since the plane's disappearance meant that there was really very little chance of anyone still being alive.

But Hal Hunt knew his brother too well.

'If he survived the crash then he's still alive,' he'd said to Amazon, back in Prince Rupert. 'And if he's alive then I'm going to find him.'

'I still don't understand why Uncle Roger and Aunt Ling-Mei didn't come back by themselves,' said

Frazer. 'I mean, they could have found a ranger station, or a hunting party, or just made their own way back to civilization by themselves, couldn't they?'

'I think you underestimate just how much wilderness there is out here, Frazer,' replied Hal. 'But I don't think it's just that. I've got a feeling that either Roger didn't want to be rescued, or someone stopped him from being rescued. Either way, the answer to this riddle is in the wreckage of their aircraft and we're going to find it, if it's the last thing TRACKS ever does.'

And so three separate teams of TRACKS young conservationists were out in the forests searching, while Dr Drexler, the TRACKS chief scientific officer, stayed back in Prince Rupert, coordinating their actions.

'OK, guys, let's focus,' said Hal Hunt, still smiling about his son's encounter with the wolverine. 'We're here to find my brother and Ling-Mei, not to horse around.'

He beckoned Frazer and Amazon to gather round, and then unfolded a map of the Canadian province of British Columbia on a low camp table.

'We're here,' he said, 'in the foothills of the Coast Range, with the heights to the west and the interior plateau to the east. Miranda Coverdale is leading a team here, further south, and Bluey's team are up here, to the north.'

Miranda and Bluey were two members of TRACKS. Bluey, named for his bright red hair, was Frazer's best friend. He was in his early twenties and had a PhD in marine biology, but he still looked and, at times, acted like a big kid. Miranda was the deputy veterinary officer to Dr Drexler. She was about the same age as Bluey, but she looked and behaved a lot older. She was definitely the sensible one in the gang.

'Tomorrow morning you two take your bikes along this trail, here. That'll take you to the foot of this hill.' Hal jabbed his finger at the map, and then pointed to a rocky outcrop in the middle distance. 'It's called Mount Humboldt, but it's more of a hill than a mountain.'

'Humboldt?' said Amazon. 'You mean like the squid . . .?'

Amazon had recently had an uncomfortably close encounter with a horde of ravenous Humboldt squid in the Pacific Ocean.

'That's right,' replied Hal, 'named after the same guy, the great German naturalist and explorer Alexander von Humboldt. He discovered –'

'There're trails?' said Frazer, before his dad could launch into one of his lectures.

'What? Oh yep. Not many. A few old hunting trails and maybe a disused logging road in the woods too. Rough, but should be OK for mountain bikes. It's twelve miles away, but the trail heads straight there, so it shouldn't take you more than two hours. Then scale Humboldt – you won't need climbing gear, it's nothing more than a hike, really – and see what you can see. From the top you'll have a view over the whole area. Obviously there's no cellphone signal out here, but we can keep in touch using the sat phones.'

'Which way are you going, Dad?'

'I'm heading out east from here, along this valley.' He traced the blue line of a river with his finger. 'If Roger was lost and flying without navigation equipment, he might have been following the river to try to reach a settlement. OK, we all clear?'

Amazon nodded. Just being out here and doing something made her feel better. It gave a little room for hope to grow.

'Yes, sir!' said Frazer, as enthusiastic as ever, his brush with the terrible man-eating wolverine already forgotten.

'In that case, let's go fishing.'

3
Aimlessly Holding a Stick

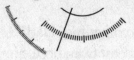

'Have you done much fishing?' Hal asked Amazon, as they walked through the woods. They were each carrying a rod and tackle.

'None,' she replied. 'Never really saw the point in standing around aimlessly holding a stick.'

'Well, honey,' said Hal, 'you'll see the point today. This isn't English fishing for minnows; this is real North American fishing. There are lake trout out there bigger than *you*.'

'Really?' said Amazon, her eyes suddenly wide. 'And what do they eat?'

'Anything smaller than them. So make sure you don't fall in!'

Amazon knew what her Uncle Hal was up to. She was desperately worried about her parents, and Hal was doing all he could to keep her mind engaged and busy so she wouldn't dwell on the dark fears that crept back whenever nothing more engrossing was there to keep them at bay.

The trouble was that this sort of thing didn't come naturally to Hal. Everything that Amazon had heard about him when he was younger from her own father created an image of a happy and relaxed person, able to enjoy life and, crucially, someone capable of standing back and letting others enjoy theirs.

But things had changed when Hal was in his early twenties. It was then that his own father, John Hunt, had been badly hurt in an accident. After that, the burden of running the business, and looking after his kid brother – Amazon's father – had fallen on Hal's young shoulders.

The spooky thing was that, although Amazon didn't know the details, she did know that he had been in a plane crash somewhere in Canada . . .

Back then they ran an operation collecting animals to sell to zoos. It was Hal at first, later helped by Roger, who changed things around and set up TRACKS, with a focus more on keeping animals safe in their own environment, rather than in zoos. He'd worked himself into the ground, sometimes travelling the world, but also doing the boring work of getting funding and lobbying governments. And so the organization had grown.

But somewhere along the way Hal had lost his joy and his zest. Where once he zipped through life, now he trudged.

The brothers finally fell out over Hal's desire to bring in ever-increasing amounts of money to pay for the TRACKS programmes around the world. Roger thought that too many compromises had been made, that TRACKS had become too close to some unsavoury governments and big corporations, which had only their own interests in mind. He thought that TRACKS had lost its soul.

And so it lost him too.

Frazer's mother had died when he was a baby, which again had heaped the pressure on his father's shoulders. He might have crumpled under it, but it just made him stronger, tougher. What it didn't make him was easy to live with. He had become closed off emotionally, reluctant to speak his heart. Frazer knew that his dad loved him, but that was because he knew how to read the signs: a half-smile here, a pat on the shoulder there.

Hal Hunt was trying with Amazon, he really was. She sensed that. But he just wasn't the person you went to when you wanted a hug and a shoulder to cry on – to lean on, yes, but not to cry on.

The trail from the campsite opened out and the crystal waters of the lake were before them. Slender pine trees rimmed the shoreline and Amazon saw a beaver lodge – an untidy mound of branches and mud – across on the far side. A single bird – a dramatic black and white Great Northern Loon – sailed serenely across the water, its wake a perfect V behind it.

The floatplane was moored close to the lakeside, near to where a spit of shingle reached out into the water like a long, bony finger. Hal led the way to the end of the spit. It was more exposed out there, with water on three sides, and Amazon shivered.

'You can feel that winter's coming,' she said.

'Another month and you'll be able to walk across to the other side,' said Hal. 'But this is still a good time for the animals. Lots to eat. And I suggest we get a modest share of it!'

'You sure there's trout out there, Dad?' said Frazer. He was already, in his mind, feasting on the fish, hot and white from the campfire.

'Oh yes,' Hal nodded. 'At this time of the year the trout come a little nearer to the surface. All summer long they've been down at the bottom, vacuuming up the baitfish. But now the water's colder, the whole crowd of 'em get a yearning for the sun.'

'How we gonna catch them, Dad. Fly?'

'Does this look like a fly rod, Frazer?' Hal answered, holding up the stout rod.

'Er, I guess not.'

'We're going to use lures.'

Hal showed Amazon how to attach the lure – a miniature model of a minnow with a cluster of hooks on its tail – to the line.

Amazon really had never fished before, and she found this part incredibly tricky. She managed to cut her finger on one of the sharp barbs, drawing a bubble of bright red blood. Hal took her hand gently in his and eased the hook out. He even had a plaster to cover up the wound.

'You're a brave kid,' Hal said. 'When Frazer here first hooked himself, he squealed so loud the fish came up to see what was happening. I do believe that a wide-mouthed bass asked if he could keep the noise down, as he was trying to get some sleep.'

'Thanks, Dad,' said Frazer, rolling his eyes. 'Got any other embarrassing stories about me? Maybe you could show Zonnie a photo of me in my diaper, sucking my thumb.'

Hal laughed one of his rare, hearty laughs. 'OK, hotshot, you can teach Amazon how to cast. I'm going to find a quiet spot further down the shore. The person that catches the biggest fish gets to eat the eyeballs.'

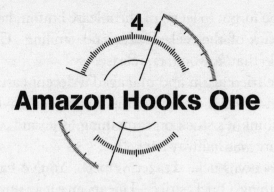

4

Amazon Hooks One

'Your dad gives you a hard time, doesn't he?' said Amazon, after Hal had walked the length of the spit and disappeared behind a fold in the shore.

'It's just his way,' replied Frazer, not looking back at his cousin.

Before Amazon had the chance to ask him any more questions, he pulled the rod back over his shoulder and sent a cast out fifteen metres into the deepest part of the lake, the lure sailing over the water in a perfect arc.

'Sweet!' said Amazon, genuinely impressed.

Frazer quickly reeled in the line, jiggling the rod so that the lure would imitate the random movements of a fish.

'Your turn,' he said, when the lure came back empty.

He showed Amazon how to hold the rod and operate the reel. She tried to copy his cast, but the lure refused to budge from the end of her rod.

'You forgot to let go of the release button, here at the back of the reel,' Frazer said, smiling. 'Unless you do that, it won't, er, release.'

She tried again and managed a decent cast. She began to reel it in, again imitating Frazer's style.

'I think it's stuck on something,' she said, when the lure was halfway back. 'I –'

'It's not stuck,' Frazer yelped. 'You've caught something. Quick, strike – I mean, give it an upwards yank, before it slips off.'

Amazon did just that, and felt the weight of the fish on the line.

'I don't believe it,' smiled Frazer. 'On your very first cast! OK, just reel it the rest of the way in, nice and slowly.'

When the fish was almost at the shore, Frazer showed Amazon how to raise the rod, lifting the lure clear of the water. And there, caught on one of the hooks, was a glistening fish, perhaps fifteen centimetres long.

Amazon let out a squeal of pure joy.

'I never thought I'd catch one in a million years!' she said, and she would have done a little fish dance if no one had been there to watch.

Frazer showed Amazon how to take the hook out of the little trout's mouth. Then she held the fish in her hands for a few seconds, taking in the perfect, speckled beauty of it.

'Hate to tell you this, Zonnie,' said Frazer, 'but we've got to throw that little fella back.'

'No! Why?'

'Too small.'

'Really?' Amazon's shoulders sagged a little, but another part of her was pleased to be able to let the beautiful creature go.

'Can't believe you hooked him with that big lure. Got to give them a chance to spawn. But now you've got the hang of it there'll be no stopping you.'

Frazer was right. In half an hour they'd caught three decent-sized trout. Frazer's was the biggest – almost as long as his arm – but Amazon had two that stretched from her hand to her elbow. She held one up and Frazer photographed it.

'One to show your mum and dad,' he said, 'when we find them.'

Amazon responded with a warm smile. It was a smile that Frazer hadn't seen her unleash before.

And then Amazon stopped smiling. For a moment Frazer thought it was because he'd mentioned her parents, which had brought back bad memories. Then he realized that Amazon wasn't even looking at him, and that her expression could only mean one thing: there was something extraordinary just behind him, standing on the narrow spit of land, right between the two of them and the safety of the shore.

He turned and there before him was a sight that filled him in equal parts with wonder, awe and terror.

5

Beautiful Danger

It was the sheer beauty of the creature that first struck Frazer. During the years he had been travelling the world with TRACKS, he had seen many bears – polar bears in Greenland, black bears and grizzlies in America, and their Asiatic cousins in the Russian Far East. He had seen sloth bears in India, greedily shovelling wasp larvae out of a nest. He had seen spectacled bears in Peru, and sun bears in Burma; but he had never seen anything like this.

Well, that wasn't *quite* true. The shape was familiar – the rounded back end, the lack of an obvious hump between the shoulder blades, the long face and the alert ears. But the colour was astonishing: a lovely pale yellow, like a jar of honey held up to the sunlight.

Just for a split second the pale colour fooled Frazer into thinking that this might be a polar bear that had somehow strayed far from its frozen homeland. But the colour was a shade too dark, and the general shape of the bear just plain wrong.

No, this was a black bear, for sure. It just wasn't, well, black.

Had the bear been on its own, Frazer would have been wary, but not scared. It was the creature behind the big bear that made him rigid with fear.

The baby.

The cub was even more enchanting than the mother: a fluffy, roly-poly ball of energy and joy, the same lovely honey colour as its mother. As Frazer watched, it tripped over its own feet, let out a little roar, looked around to see who had noticed its mishap and then ran up to snuggle at its mother's ample behind.

Cute.

But this was the one situation that all naturalists feared most: a mother bear with her cub. It transformed a relatively harmless creature – most species of bear would much rather hunt mice than men – into a potential killer.

'DO NOT MOVE!'

The voice that rang out was so full of authority that it seemed that even the mother bear obeyed it. Frazer looked up and saw his father further along the shore. Hal's face appeared quite calm, but Frazer saw – or sensed – the tension beneath his skin, and he realized just how worried his father was. That in itself was enough to raise Frazer's fear factor by a couple of notches.

'All she wants are the fish,' said Hal Hunt, his voice

now soft and soothing. Frazer realized how hard he was trying to maintain that veneer of calmness. 'Throw them towards her, and then wade out to the plane and get in. Stay there till the bears leave. Got that?'

Frazer nodded. He checked out Amazon. He was expecting to see her face frozen in terror, but in fact it was shining with a radiant light.

'They're so beautiful,' she said. 'I didn't know that there were bears that colour . . .'

'OK, Zonnie,' said Frazer, 'we can wax lyrical about those guys when we're safe. For now, we give them our dinner and get the heck out of harm's way. One swipe of that paw and we're as dead as that big trout you've got there.'

Amazon snapped out of her trance. The three trout they'd caught were at her feet. She picked one up and threw it towards the mother bear. It flopped on to the ground in front of her, and she took a step towards it and sniffed. Frazer threw the other two fish. The bear squatted down, put her big paws on the spotted flesh and began to gorge. The little one emerged from behind her and joined in with the feast.

'Right,' said Frazer, 'just follow me.'

The floatplane was moored five metres off the spit, at a point opposite where the bears were now busy eating. Frazer's plan was to circle round to the far side of the aircraft and get in. He knew, as did his father, that they'd be safe in there.

He took Amazon's hand, and together they backed into the water, not taking their eyes off the bears. The water was soon up to their knees, and they began to edge their way round to the plane.

And then Frazer stumbled on a submerged tree branch. He splashed into the cold water and let out an involuntary gasp. The mother bear leapt to her feet and emitted a harsh bark, almost like a dog. She began to bustle towards the two Trackers, as Amazon helped Frazer back to his feet.

'HA! HERE!' yelled Hal Hunt from the shore, trying to get the bear's attention. She spun to face him, pushing the cub behind her defensively. The sight of the big human made her forget the two smaller ones. He was more of a threat to her baby. Hal began to make soothing noises, and slowly walked backwards, making it clear to the bear that he had no predatory intentions towards the cub.

'Quick,' hissed Frazer, 'while she's not looking . . .'

Not even trying to be careful, they splashed noisily towards the floatplane. The water was now waist-deep. Amazon felt as though it were made of treacle, it seemed to grab and suck at her so. And, even though it was only a few metres to safety, she found it utterly exhausting.

Frazer made it to the plane first, and hauled himself up on to the float, which made the whole fragile aircraft rock in the water. He dragged Amazon dripping from the lake, and wrenched open the door.

Amazon looked back over her shoulder, convinced that she was going to see the bear pounding after them. The mother, however, was still glaring at Hal, guarding the cub between her massive front paws.

Amazon slammed the door behind her, and suddenly felt completely safe. Something about the look of the busy console with its dials and switches, the joystick, that earlier today her Uncle Hal had gripped to guide them here, even the smell of the plastic seats, just felt so civilized. The worn and familiar interior banished the idea that it was even remotely possible that she could be killed by an angry bear in the wilds of Canada.

They both glanced out of the grimy window. The mother and cub were now tucking into the fish, looking very relaxed. Hal had retreated further, and was squatting down on his haunches, observing the scene.

'That was pretty, er, tense,' said Frazer.

'Yeah, I could hardly bear it . . .' said Amazon with a slight smile creeping across her face.

Frazer looked at her. 'That is the worst joke I've ever heard, and hanging out with Bluey means that I've heard a fair few,' he said, but his mouth was already twitching. The joke hit their funny bones like a sledgehammer, and they both started first to giggle, and then they burst out into peals of laughter.

'If you're so clever, you think of a better bear joke,' gasped Amazon.

Frazer wiped his eyes on his sleeve. 'OK,' he said, 'I've got one for you. There's a bear and a rabbit walking together through the woods. The bear's looking thoughtful. He says to the rabbit, "Do you have trouble with poop sticking to your fur?" "Nope," says his little friend. "That's good," says the bear and wipes his butt with the rabbit.'

That set them off again, and it was a couple of minutes before they thought to look out of the window to check on the bears' meal.

The mother and cub had finished the three trout they'd been thrown. Now the mother was sniffing the air, her nose held high.

'Guess she's still hungry,' said Frazer.

And then, to their dismay, the big female began to wade out towards the floatplane.

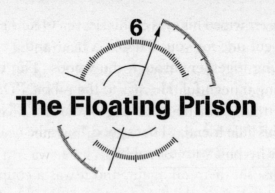

6

The Floating Prison

'This is not good,' said Frazer.

'Where's your dad gone?' asked Amazon. She'd just noticed that Hal Hunt was no longer watching them.

Before Frazer had the chance to answer, the bear reached the plane. She disappeared from their view for a moment as she clambered up clumsily on to the float and then her huge head reared up right in the window. Amazon and Frazer both managed to strangle their screams, but they could not resist the primal need to cling on to each other.

The bear shoved her nose against the window and sniffed.

'I don't get it,' said Frazer. 'We're no threat to her or her baby while we're in here. This isn't usual bear behaviour at all. Unless . . .'

'Unless what?'

'Well, I suppose it's possible that she's not really

concerned about her cub's safety. She might just be hungry and sees us as the second course.'

'But surely bears don't eat people . . .?'

'Nope, not usually. Mice and berries are more their thing. But there are times when a bear just decides that it wants to try something new.'

It was then that Hal came back. He was carrying his rifle.

'Your dad's not going to shoot the bear, is he?' said Amazon, her face full of apprehension.

'No! Well, I hope not. It would only be if we were in real danger.'

'But you just said that the bear might want to eat us . . .'

'Yeah, but I don't think the bear can . . .'

Frazer was going to say, 'get in here', but then the bear started beating on the door of the plane with those powerful clawed feet.

The whole plane began to rock from side to side again, and now it was impossible for the two young Trackers not to scream. The sound just seemed to encourage the bear. Amazon saw Hal step forward. He pulled back the bolt in the old rifle, chambering a round.

And then Frazer saw it sticking up out of the top of one of the big pockets on Amazon's jacket.

'Zonnie, is that what I think it is?' he said, pointing at the protruding tail.

'What? Oh well, I . . . look, it was the first time I've ever been fishing, and I didn't want to give *everything* to the bears. I just wanted one to show . . .'

Frazer didn't wait for her to finish. He just pulled the fish from her pocket and jumped into the back seat of the aircraft. From there he pulled open one of the windows. The bear's head shot in his direction. He waved the fish in front of her nose, and then hurled it out into the lake. The bear dived straight after it, sending out a wave that rocked the little plane.

'Now!' Frazer yelled. 'Run for it.'

Together they jumped from the plane and splashed to the shore. Hal ran to meet them. The little cub, still halfway up the spit, gave a fierce little roar in their direction, which brought the mother bear thundering back.

'OK, we back off,' said Hal, still holding the gun, ready to fire. 'Nice and slow.'

The others didn't need any further instruction. Staying close together, they edged away from the lake and the bears and, unharassed by the grumpy mum, they stumbled back to camp.

7

The Spirit Bears

'That was a lucky escape,' Hal Hunt said later in camp as they slurped thin packet soup from tin mugs.

'I think we had it covered,' said Frazer.

'I meant a lucky escape for the bear. If I'd had to then I would have shot her. And that would have made this one depressing trip.'

'I've never seen bears like those two,' said Amazon, trying to change the subject. She couldn't stand the thought of her uncle killing the bears all because of her fishy mistake. 'They were such an amazing colour. Are they albinos?'

'No, not an albino. True albinos always have pink eyes,' said Hal. 'They're actually a subspecies of black bear that we get here in British Columbia. They're usually called Kermode bears, but the First Nation people call them spirit bears, which I kind of like. It's because they look like ghosts. But it's just a genetic mutation. They're not at all common, and they usually live down by the coast – haven't seen any this far inland before.'

By now the sun had set, and it was getting cold. Hal put another log on the fire.

'You must have been up here a lot with Uncle Roger back in the old days,' said Frazer. He was thinking that Amazon might like to hear some stories about her dad.

Hal nodded, but didn't, as Frazer expected, launch into some funny stories about the scrapes he and his brother had got into. And then Hal cleared his throat and began to talk.

8

Hal Hunt's Tale

'I never told you, did I, about how your grandfather, my dad, John Hunt, almost died? Well, it was north of here, up near the border with Alaska. You won't like the sound of this, but we were up there collecting bald eagle eggs. No, hold your horses, it was all to help save the species. The birds had once been common all over North America, but they were down to just a few hundred pairs.

'Scientists had found that a pesticide called DDT was making their eggshells very thin and delicate, and so when the parents tried to brood the eggs they would break. So we were up there to try to collect some eggs for a captive breeding programme. And, if you got the eggs early in the season, the eagles would lay a second clutch, so the species wouldn't be harmed at all. But yes, I suppose that we'd do things differently now. This was back in the days when we didn't know as much as we do now about conservation.

'Anyway, my dad was piloting us in a floatplane, pretty similar to the one I flew you guys here in. There was just Dad, Roger and me in the plane. We were planning to be up there for three or four days at the most. We had an incubator that would keep the eggs viable till we got back to New England.

'We'd set off from Vancouver early in the morning. The weather was fine, no problems there at all. And then my dad noticed that the fuel gauge was almost on empty. We should have had plenty of gas to get us there and back. He reckoned that there was a leak.

'This was pretty bad news. It meant that he was going to have to set us down in one of the lakes up there, and then we were going to have to trek back hundreds of miles to civilization. And we hadn't come prepared for that kind of expedition. But we weren't too worried. In fact, Roger and I were excited about it. It was going to feel like a real adventure, out there hundreds of miles from anywhere, having to live off the land and our wits. And with dad there too . . . You see, most of the time Dad just sent Roger and me off round the world on our own, so we hardly ever got to spend this sort of time with him.

'But then, when I looked at my dad, I saw that he was worried. He was a cool character, old John Hunt. But he wasn't cool, then. The sweat was dripping down his face. He was looking for somewhere safe to put the plane down. We went over a couple of small lakes, but there just wasn't enough room for us to land safely. By now the gauge was reading nothing but a big red zero.

'Your dad, Amazon, was still laughing and joking, because that was his way, but me and my dad knew better. He managed to nurse the plane over one more ridge of pines – we were so close the floats clipped the branches at the top. And there below us was a lovely long lake. Could have been made for landing a plane on. I remember it now, still and shiny as a river of mercury.

'I saw my dad's face relax. He even smiled, and said to Roger that we'd be fishing that evening in the lake. He couldn't gain any height, but the prop was still turning.

'We only had a mile or so to go when she stalled. Just dropped down the last fifteen metres and hit the trees. It felt like the end of the world. The wings got torn off, and the fuselage cracked in two like someone breaking an egg to make an omelette.

'We'd belted up, of course, and that saved my life. I woke up later – guess it was only a few minutes – and I didn't know what the heck had happened or where I was. I didn't even understand what I was seeing. You see, the plane had flipped over, and I was hanging upside down. Roger was next to me, just coming round. I checked him quickly, and he seemed to be OK, just stunned by the crash.

'And then I saw my dad, down below me on the forest floor, and I knew straight away that he was seriously injured, because of the way he was lying, all twisted up.

'I managed to rouse Roger, and we climbed down out of those trees. We were both pretty shaken up, and it's a miracle that we got down in one piece.

'And then Roger saw the state that Dad was in, and that bust him up. Your father took it badly, Amazon. He was only a kid, whereas I was already a man.'

Amazon was so caught up in the story she didn't know what to say. In her mind she was there in the crash, with Roger and Hal and old John Hunt.

'How badly hurt was he?' asked Frazer.

'Dad was out cold – he'd taken a nasty crack to the head. He also had a compound fracture to his leg – his shin bone was sticking out through his torn trouser leg. Roger was panicking, freaking out. I told him to go and get two stout branches and trim them off with his knife – we were going to need them to splint the leg, but I also wanted to give him something to do while I worked on the injury.

'A compound fracture is just about the worst thing that can happen when you're out in the wilderness. This was a bad break, but it could have been worse. The bone looked like a broken stick, all jagged and white, but by some miracle the shards hadn't cut through any major blood vessels so, although it was bleeding, it wasn't, well, gushing.

'Normally the advice is to do what you can to stem

any bleeding, but then wait till the medics turn up to fix it. Most of the things an amateur could do to a compound fracture would make it worse. You shouldn't touch the bone, because all that'll do is damage the flesh around it more and get the whole thing infected. But there were no medics out there, so it was down to me. Luckily I'd read up on first aid, so I had a rough idea what to do.

'We had plenty of bottled water, and a medical kit with decent supplies in it. The kit had fallen out of the plane not far from my dad. So first of all I dissolved an iodine tablet in a bottle of water and used that to flush out the wound, which was full of leaf mould and general crud.

'Then it was time for the hard part. I knew that we had a serious trek ahead of us if we were going to get my dad out alive, and I couldn't leave the bone just sticking out like that – the wound would never heal, and the infection would kill him.

'Roger was back by now. He was still upset, but he knew as well as I did that we had to keep cool and sort this out. I asked him to hold tight on to Dad's shoulders, while I pulled on the foot. I managed to get the bone to slide back the way it had come, and settle more or less in the right place. If I'd messed it up, the sharp edge of the bone would have caused more tissue damage, and maybe even nicked an artery. Thank God Dad was still unconscious. It would have hurt like hell if he'd been awake. In fact, the pain might have been enough to send him into shock and kill him.

'We had some bandages in the med kit, so I cleaned and dressed the wound as best I could. Then I used more bandage to tie the two branches to Dad's leg. It was important, you see, to keep the leg immobile – any movement of the bone would be a disaster.

'After that, I went back up into the trees and threw down anything useful – we had a little food and some camping gear – and a couple of guns; there was a rifle and my dad's Colt 45 that he'd had in the army.

'By then it was too late to begin our journey back to civilization, so that night we camped by the lake. Dad woke up in the night, which was a big relief. Except that he was in terrible pain from that leg, and he didn't make much sense. He said that we should leave him up there and get back ourselves, and then send a party back for him. But we both knew that they'd find him dead, and I wasn't going to let that happen.

'The next morning we rigged up a travois – you know, a sort of sledge made out of branches – and tied my dad to it. Then we began to walk. Every step was agony for my dad, but he never complained beyond the occasional grunt.

'I had a map and a compass, and I was always pretty good at finding my way around. We headed for the Anchorage to Newport Road, which I reckoned was about fifty miles away. I thought we'd be able to catch a lift from there. It took us four days. The going was as rough as it gets. There was never a time when we weren't dragging that sledge up or hauling it down – in fact, going down was sometimes harder than going up, because we didn't want to lose control and drop our dad.

'The second night – the first of the journey – was OK. Dad was still in terrible pain, and was drifting in and out of consciousness. He had a few lucid moments, and we talked through our plans. I could tell he was proud of the way we were coping – especially Roger, who, as I keep saying, was just a kid – pretty much the same age as you, Frazer.'

Amazon looked at her cousin and tried to imagine her dad at the same age. It made her smile, despite the grimness of the story.

'I checked Dad's leg,' continued Hal. 'The bandages were caked with dried blood, and it must have hurt like hell when I peeled them off. The wound didn't look too bad, but I thought I caught the smell of something . . . well, something not good. I flushed it with iodine again, and Dad made a sort of deep animal sound in his throat, and he punched at the ground, and Roger tried to hold him still.

'The trouble started the next day. We heard wolves howling in the night, but we never thought too much about it. We knew that there were almost no cases of humans being attacked by wolves in modern times. It just didn't happen. Bears, yes, but not wolves. Also, well, Dad was always a big wolf guy. There were always wolves back on the farm, then, and we just didn't think about wolves as being anything other than our friends.

'But we hadn't reckoned on a couple of things. It was spring, after a long, hard winter, and the wolves had cubs, so they needed food. A lot of food. And my dad, well, the wolves could sense that he was sick.

'They are magnificent hunters, but there's not a single predator out there that doesn't prefer to chow down on something that's already on the way out.

'Anyway, the wolves tracked us all that day. We never saw them once, but we knew they were there. They didn't howl on the chase, but there was something about the forest that just screamed out *wolves*.

'That night they howled again. We built the fire up and I think that kept them away. Dad was hot. Despite the iodine, an infection had taken hold and he was getting feverish. He'd stopped making much sense. He talked a lot about our mom, which he never did normally. She'd died when we were little kids. And it wasn't just that he was talking *about* her – he was talking *to* her. And, well, that was pretty tough for Roger too . . .

'Day three we saw them. A line of seven big timber wolves up on a ridge. The leader was as black as night. In fact, it looked like a wolf-shaped chunk of night had broken off and slipped into the day. And it looked at me. Right at me. It was too far off for me to see its eyes, but I knew it was looking at me. It was looking into my soul, to see if I had the courage and the will to protect our burden. And when the wolf looked at me I knew I'd be bringing Dad home or I'd die trying.

'The next night I built up a fire so big you could have seen it from space. And I did something else. I stayed beside it all night. I didn't want the wolves slinking down to the tent, with me inside. So I sat there with the Colt 45 in my hand. The rifle – it was this same one here – was, as you can see, a single-shot, bolt-action gun, and I needed something that could shoot a lot faster than that. Plus, the range was going to be close, so I didn't need the accuracy of a rifle.

'Anyway, I sat with my back to the fire. I heard Roger talking to Dad, trying to soothe him to sleep, and I watched the stars come out, and then the moon rise, but it was only a sliver, like a fingernail held up to a candle. I was wrapped in a blanket, and had the gun on my lap.

'And, although I was determined to stay awake, I fell asleep. One second I was awake, the next, dreaming. I don't know what it was that woke me up, maybe an owl hooting – well, whatever, but whatever it was it saved my life. Because there, right in front of me, was the leader of the wolf pack – the big black wolf, like something out of a fairy tale or a nightmare. And he was so perfectly still, had it not been for the last of the flames from my fire reflected back from his eyes, making them look like the red eyes of a demon, I would never have seen him. And I reached down and picked up the Colt 45, and I pointed it at the wolf.'

'Did you shoot him, Dad?' asked Frazer, his eyes wide and glimmering in the light of the fire.

Hal was silent for a few seconds, and then he continued. 'I pointed the gun at the wolf and I pulled the trigger. But I hadn't taken off the safety. Schoolboy error. It hardly made a sound – the pistol, I mean – when I tried to fire it with the safety on. But somehow it startled the wolf, and it leapt away.

'I don't know why, but I have a feeling it had been there for a long time, watching me, trying to figure out who I was. It could have killed me pretty easily, I guess. And the fact that it could have killed me, and didn't, and that I tried to kill it, and failed, well, that changed me. From that day to this I've never killed another animal, except for a fish for the pan.

'The next day the wolves stayed with us, but I never felt the same threat from them. I left some of our food behind at the campsite as a kind of offering, so maybe they were just following us to get some more.

'Anyway, late that day we hit a logging road. We got lucky – a truck came along after a couple of hours. The trucker was this French Canadian guy.

He couldn't believe what we'd done. By that stage my dad was completely out of it. At first the trucker didn't want to take my dad in the truck with us because he said he was drunk. But Roger, well, Roger just blew a gasket. He took the rifle and said that he was going to shoot the French Canadian guy in the leg if he didn't take us straight to the nearest hospital.

'The trucker just looked at Roger. He didn't even blink. He wasn't afraid, but he agreed. I guess he got the message. So then he drove us back to Anchorage.

'My dad was in the hospital there for three months. The infection had gotten into the bone and it was all they could do to save the leg. He walked with a limp from then until the day he died. He still did what he could to help us with our conservation projects, but he wasn't the same man, and basically, from the moment of the crash, it was me and Roger together against the bad guys.'

There was a long silence after Hal Hunt stopped speaking. Then Frazer cleared his throat.

'Gee, Dad, I've never heard you talk about that before. I guess it explains a lot.'

'No, son, it doesn't explain anything. It's just a thing that happened. I . . . we . . . moved on. Talking of which, we've got work to do tomorrow, so I suggest we all get some shut-eye.'

It was cold in the night. Amazon and Frazer slept with their clothes on. In the night Amazon woke up.

'Frazer,' she said quietly to see if her cousin was awake. When she got no response, she pinched him. 'Frazer!'

'Huh?'

'Did you hear that?'

'What? I was asleep . . . what are you asking?'

'I thought I heard something.'

'What sort of thing?'

I don't know. Moving. Noises. A bear, maybe.'

'Nah – we tied all the food up in a tree away from the camp. There won't be any bears. Go to sleep.'

'Wait – there again. That noise.'

Now Frazer heard it too.

'It doesn't sound like any animal I know,' he said softly. 'But it's probably just a deer, or racoon. Or maybe a skunk.' Deep down he had a slight fear that it might be the wolverine, come for a second chance at biting his butt. He'd rather face a bear any day.

'Will you have a look, Frazer?' Amazon pleaded. She was spooked, and Frazer knew that the only way to free someone of an irrational fear – hers of the bear, his of the wolverine – was with knowledge, with light. He took the torch from his pack, and carefully undid the ties fastening the tent flap. Amazon crouched behind him.

Then, without warning, Frazer began to crawl out into the night. Amazon grabbed him.

'Fraze, where are you going? What animal is it?'

'It's my dad. He's crying. I think it's about your dad. And I reckon I'm going to give him a hug.'

Amazon drifted off to sleep to the sound of her cousin and uncle talking quietly beside the fire. And as she fell asleep she found hope in the story of the rescue. Like Roger and Hal Hunt, she would bring her own parents back from the wilderness.

9

The Message

It wasn't the sun streaming through the thin material of the tent that woke Amazon the next morning. It was the anxious sound of Hal Hunt's voice outside, and the crackle of another voice coming in over the sat phone.

'You're sure? A Kermode bear . . .? And it definitely killed the boy . . .? Oh, I see. So they haven't found . . . Wait, let me get those coordinates down. Yep, that's not far from here. I can hike there in a couple of hours. Thanks, Drex. Goodbye.'

Amazon shook Frazer awake, and they crawled out of the tent. Hal Hunt was already busy cramming a small daypack with supplies.

'What's happening, Dad?' asked Frazer, wiping the sleep from his eyes.

'Trouble,' said Hal, his face stern and grim. 'A group of hikers were out in the mountains not far from here. Last night they were attacked at their campsite. There was mayhem. Three of them were badly injured. There was a child with them – a six-year-old boy, out on his first camping trip. He's . . . well, he disappeared. His parents, as you can imagine, were distraught. They searched everywhere for him, although they themselves were among those injured by the bear. They were picked up by a Canadian Mounted Police patrol this morning and flown out.'

Amazon cut in: 'You said it was a spirit bear that attacked the campers?'

'A Kermode bear, that's right.'

'But surely not the mother we saw with the cub yesterday?'

'No, I doubt that very much. It was too far away. And, besides, the campers spoke of a huge bear. They would have said that it was a grizzly if it hadn't been for the colour. But that won't save her.'

'Why?' cried Amazon. 'What do you mean?'

'Word about the attack has gone back to Prince Rupert and the other settlements, and every hunter around is going to be out here soon looking for spirit bears to shoot. A child has been killed, and there is going to be a price to pay.'

'But that's not right!' said Frazer. 'They can't just shoot any old bear, can they?'

'You're forgetting what people are like. They want revenge. They want blood.'

'Isn't there anything we can do?' said Amazon. She was already in a fury at the thought of what might happen to 'her' bears, the beautiful mother and baby.

'Yes, there is,' said Hal, his face somehow finding an even deeper level of gravity. 'I'm going to find and kill the bear that did this.'

'No!' screamed Amazon. 'You said you'd never kill another animal . . .'

'But, Dad,' added Frazer, his voice cracked with astonishment and horror, 'you can't . . . There must be another way.'

Hal Hunt shook his head.

'Unless I get that bear – the right bear – then every Kermode bear in this province is going to be slaughtered. Finding the killer is the only way to save the rest of the species.'

Frazer and Amazon both, reluctantly, saw the strength of the argument – and the pain it was causing Hal Hunt.

'OK, Dad,' said Frazer. 'I'll get packing.'

'No.'

'What?'

'You're staying here. It's too dangerous out there with a killer bear on the prowl. And besides,' he continued over the top of Frazer's groan, 'I'll move more quickly on my own. If I can find the bear today then I can destroy it and get word back before any innocent bears are killed. I'll check in every few hours on the sat phone – and you call me if anything happens here. Oh, that reminds me, the battery on the other sat phone is pretty low. Stick it in the solar charger and it'll be good to go in a couple of hours.'

Fifteen minutes later, Hal marched from the camp, calling out his last instructions.

'I don't think the bear will come in this direction, but I don't want to take any chances. So I'd like you two to stay in the plane. It's not so important during the day, but that's where I want you at night. Got that?'

'Yeah,' they both said, a little reluctantly.

'I mean it. The bear that killed the kid . . . he just rampaged through the campsite, tearing everything up.'

'We'll stay in the plane, Uncle Hal,' said Amazon.

Hal looked at her, gave a brief, anguished smile and disappeared into the woods.

10

The News is Bad

The world – the great blue canopy above them, the deep green of the endless conifer forest, the black mountains and white peaks – seemed very silent after Hal Hunt had gone. Amazon and Frazer looked at each other.

'What do we do now?' Amazon asked.

'We wait,' Frazer replied. 'And we fish.'

'*Seriously?* You can't mean it . . .'

Amazon had been hoping – in fact, expecting – that Frazer would never agree just to sit around and wait. He was usually as irrepressible as a typhoon. Surely he'd be up for taking the bikes on a reconnaissance mission . . .?

'But my mum and dad,' she said, trying not to let her voice turn into a whine. 'We could take the bikes and –'

'I promised my dad, Amazon,' replied Frazer, not meeting her fervent gaze. 'You know me, I like to do . . . *stuff*. If there's wiggle room then I wiggle. But

Dad made me promise, and I'm going to stick to it. The thing about my dad is that he always keeps his word. And, because of that, it's no fun at all when you break yours to him.'

'But I just feel . . . *useless*,' said Amazon. 'I'll go mad if we just hang around here doing nothing. I have this feeling that my parents are out there, just beyond my reach. It's agonizing.'

Frazer put his arm round her and squeezed. Because he was usually such a doofus, she kept forgetting how strong he was, for a kid.

'Look, my dad will be here tomorrow. Then we can get back on the case. I told you – he keeps his word. Now with some people that just means that they don't tell lies. But with my dad it's not a passive thing like that – I mean, just not doing something bad. It means that what he says he'll do, he does. He said he'll find your parents, so he will. End of story. Now,' Frazer continued as he hooked up the sat phone's USB connector to the large black solar panel that charged it, 'let's see if you can remember how to catch a trout.'

The fishing wasn't great. They sat on the fat, cylindrical floats of the plane and dangled their rods (and their feet) in the placid waters. Amazon managed a spiny little number that she thought looked, with its glittering red scales and iridescent blue fins, rather beautiful. But Frazer shook his head dismissively.

'Junk fish,' he said, unhooked it and threw it back. 'Full of bones.'

The highlight of the morning was a visit from a huge eagle. The eagle's body was a rich dark brown, streaked with golden highlights, but its head was clothed in pure white.

'Look at that!' exclaimed Amazon. 'That's a bald eagle, isn't it? The same kind of bird Uncle Hal was helping.'

'Sure is,' replied Frazer. 'They've made an amazing comeback. Like Dad said, they were down to just a few hundred pairs in the whole country, but now there are at least fifty thousand. It's all because they banned that pesticide, DDT – the one my dad talked about.'

'I've never seen one, except on the TV,' said Amazon.

And then she thought of all the animals she'd seen in 'real life' since she'd become a Tracker just a few months ago: tigers, leopards, bears, sea turtles, sharks. It was a dream come true, and she smiled to herself wonderingly.

As they watched, the eagle flapped majestically across the lake, then swooped down and hooked a fish with one foot.

'That's the way to do it,' said Frazer.

But he spoke too soon. The fish was a big one, and it writhed and squirmed in a way that suggested that it very much didn't want to leave its own element.

The eagle tried to get its other set of claws round the fish, but failed, and the fish – a lake trout like the ones they'd sacrificed to the bears – splashed back down into the water.

The eagle seemed genuinely enraged by this whole business, and plunged back down after it. This time its descent was too steep to allow for the sort of delicate plucking manoeuvre that had caught the trout the first time. The bird went hurtling straight into the lake. There was a flurry of feathers and a flash of scales in the sunlight, and then the eagle hauled itself by sheer might out of the grip of the water and back into the air, carrying the fish securely this time in both sets of iron talons.

Amazon was still gasping at the drama of all this when she heard something she really wasn't expecting: music. She turned round and saw Frazer sitting in the pilot seat of the plane. He stuck his head out of the window.

'Totally forgot that there's a radio in here,' he said, grinning. 'Makes it all seem a bit less lonely, doesn't it?'

Amazon was going to say that the raucous sound of pop music just didn't seem right in this beautiful, pristine wilderness. But then the music finished, and the radio station – a local Canadian one – went to the news bulletin.

' . . . *teams of Canadian Mounted Police are still searching for Ben Waits, the child missing following the brutal bear attack in the early hours of this morning . . .*'

'Hey,' said Frazer, 'that's –'

'I know what it is. And shush, I'm trying to listen!'

'. . . *described by one of the survivors as a "white monster, like something from a nightmare". The search is centred on an area south of Mount Humboldt, where the party was camping before the attack. The state authorities have discouraged the groups of hunters who are approaching the area, saying that this is only likely to impede the search. In other news, The St Edward's Island Redbacks lost a . . .*'

Frazer turned the radio off. 'I hope my dad finds that rogue bear,' he said. 'Or maybe I hope he doesn't, if it really *is* a monster.'

Amazon, however, wasn't really listening to Frazer. Something about the news report wriggled away in the back of her mind, like a worm on a hook.

'Where's the map, Frazer?' she asked.

'Back at the campsite. Why?'

'I don't know. Something . . .'

A few minutes later, the two of them were bent over the map.

'That news bulletin said south of Mount Humboldt, didn't it?'

'Er, I can't remember. Maybe.'

'Well, I do remember, and it did. That's where we were supposed to go and look for my parents. But your dad has gone north, hasn't he?'

Frazer's face went blank, and then wrinkled in puzzlement. 'Yeah, he did. My dad must have got confused somehow. That's unusual – he's normally a pretty together guy when it comes to directions. Maybe he misheard . . .?'

'Well, it doesn't matter why he went the wrong way, but went the wrong way he sure did,' said Amazon. 'Can you get your dad on the sat phone?'

'I'm on it.'

Frazer knelt by the phone, which was still attached to the black solar panel.

'Oh rats!' he spat.

'What is it?'

'I didn't plug the charger into the mini SBB socket properly. The stupid thing hasn't charged at all. In fact, now it's completely drained.'

'How long will it take before we can use it?'

Frazer gazed at the blank screen and shook his head. 'Hours.'

'We haven't got hours. That little boy's out there all alone. Well, you know what this means, don't you?'

Frazer started to smile. He knew exactly what Amazon was thinking.

'It means that we have to go to Mount Humboldt and try to find that kid.'

11

The Ride

'There's only one way to do this, you know,' said Frazer.

'The bikes,' replied Amazon, without much relish.

The bikes had been Frazer's idea, back in Prince Rupert, before they'd set out into the wilderness.

'We'll be able to cover *way* more ground than on foot,' he'd argued.

He also guessed that it might be fun.

He and Amazon had spent half a day choosing the right bikes, while the rest of the expedition was being kitted out.

'The big question is,' he'd mused, looking over the lines of beautiful bikes in the shop, 'do we go for full suspension or hardtail?'

'Shall I just pretend to know what you're talking about?' said Amazon.

'You *can* ride a bike, can't you?'

'Of course I can. I just haven't done much

mountain biking, mainly because there aren't any mountains in the area of England where I grew up.'

Amazon's own bike was rusting in a corner of her parents' garage, back in England. It was a straightforward trundler, with a shopping basket on the front, and brakes that stopped you five minutes after you started to squeeze them. But that didn't matter as the bike couldn't go much above the pace of a sloth wading through treacle.

However, Frazer was in his element. Mountain biking was just about his favourite activity in the universe.

'OK, let me run this past you quickly. I'm going to simplify this, or we'll be here all day. The basic question is, do we want something geared up for bombing downhill at maximum speed? If we do, we need full suspension. Or do we want a bike for going cross-country, with as much up as down? If so then we need to think about cutting down on weight, and that means sacrificing the rear suspension. But then that also means getting a sore butt, especially if we do actually hit a good descent.'

Amazon was already a little bored with the bike chat.

'You decide. But I'd quite like a pink one.'

'Sure . . .' said Frazer, not really listening. Then he looked up sharply and saw, from the wicked smile playing at the corners of her mouth, that this was one of Amazon's little jokes. She was not a very pink sort of girl.

In the end Frazer settled on a hardtail, matt-black Cannondale, and Amazon on a carbon-framed Marin, with full suspension.

It was a cool, metallic grey – not pink.

Back in the wilderness, they were both helmeted and ready to set off. They planned to eat a lunch of trail mix – a high-energy mixture of nuts and dried fruit, and their light backpacks also contained a few protein bars, a little chocolate and some packet soup, along with basic survival equipment in case they got into trouble.

'The last thing you want on a cross-country trip,' Frazer explained to Amazon, 'is a heavy pack. Saps all the fun out of it.'

They were both wearing standard TRACKS expedition outfits – combat trousers, a fleece and a waterproof jacket. It was enough, Frazer had said, for the daytime, when, although cool, it never got too cold. The nights were a different matter, but they had no intention of staying out at night . . .

Amazon was looking forward to the ride. But she was also a little worried. Since she had become a member of TRACKS she had been in many dangerous situations, and she knew that she had grown up and matured and that things that would have daunted her a few weeks before now seemed routine. But there was still an awful lot of wilderness out there . . .

'OK, let's move 'em out,' said Frazer, and they were off.

The first part of the ride was fairly easy. Frazer set a fast pace, but there was a good trail through the woods, and the going was pretty level. The ground was a little damp under the trees, but the heavy, knobbly tyres of the bikes bit in and gave good traction.

There were a few sections of the trail that undulated just enough for Frazer to show Amazon how to do a jump.

'You've got to pull her up,' he said, 'and make sure you land on both wheels together. The bike'll take care of the rest. Just feel it.'

Even though the bike was only airborne for a second and travelled at most a metre, it was still enough to make Amazon shriek with excitement. And fear. The landing was surprisingly easy, the suspension taking all the shock out of it.

'Told you you'd like it,' said Frazer, cycling next to her.

Amazon was exhilarated, and now the two of them flew through the forest. Sunlight filtered through the branches, dappling the ground with a lovely pattern of light and shade.

If it had not been for the seriousness of their

mission, both Amazon and Frazer would have been having fun. But the reality nagged away in the back of their minds. They were searching for a missing child. They both hoped that they would find him alive. But there was a chance, the terrible chance, that they might not . . .

After half an hour, the trail grew rougher. What had been pleasantly rolling terrain grew more rugged. There were a couple more jumps, each one higher than the one before. Amazon was delighted that her bike had full suspension, rather than just the front suspension that Frazer had – although it didn't seem to bother him. He greeted each jump with a '*Woo hoo!*', and even pulled a wheelie down one long, straight section.

'Show-off!' yelled Amazon, but she was secretly a little impressed. Impressed, that is, until he overbalanced and fell backwards with the heavy bike on top of him.

She managed not to laugh until she'd established that he wasn't badly hurt.

'You OK?' she asked as she picked him up.

'With a helmet *and* a skull this thick, I think I'll survive.' Frazer climbed back on his bike, trying to recover his dignity. 'Come on, we've work to do.'

Amazon was too busy concentrating on staying on her bike to fully appreciate the countryside, or notice any animals. Once she thought that she saw a glimpse of something large and brown moving lithely off through the undergrowth. A deer? Maybe a moose? It seemed too graceful to be a bear.

Either way, no time to ponder as she pumped the pedals to keep up with her cousin.

They stopped a couple of times to check the map. They both had watches with a GPS positioning function, so it was pretty easy to plot their route.

Amazon hadn't really been aware of it, but she now saw that they must have been climbing steadily. The trees had grown thinner, and now the Trackers were mainly cycling in sunlight rather than shade. And then for the first time she caught a glimpse of their destination: Mount Humboldt looming above them. They paused and looked at it.

It wasn't high enough to be capped with white at this time of year, but it was still a grimly impressive sight. Its sides were harsh and angular, and the grey of the rock had an almost metallic shimmer.

'How on earth are we going to get up that thing?' asked Amazon despairingly.

Frazer took the map out again.

'If you look here, you can see from the contour lines that the north face is much less steep.'

Frazer pointed to the map. 'The lines join together areas that are at the same altitude. What it means is that the closer they are together, the steeper the terrain. And see, here, on the side of the mountain we're facing, the lines are close together, but they're more widely separated on the other side. You get it?'

Amazon nodded vaguely. She had never had to read a map in her old life, back in boarding school in Sussex.

'Sure. Whatever.'

'You should try to get this stuff into your head,' replied Frazer, his voice completely lacking its usual note of playfulness.

'OK, I get it,' snapped Amazon. 'Lines close together means steep; lines not close together mean, er, not steep.'

Frazer rolled his eyes. He was actually quite enjoying being the sensible one for a change.

'The trail we're on skirts round the base of the mountain,' he continued. 'We can climb up from this point here –' He pointed at the map. 'In fact, it's not really a climb at all, more of a stroll. When we're up there, we should be able to see forever.'

'I think there may be a slight problem with your plan,' said Amazon.

'What's that?'

'Listen.'

'Listen to what?'

Amazon held up her hand. And behind the sound of the wind in the trees, and the chirruping of woodland birds, there was the distinct noise of water. Of water moving quickly.

White water.

12

The Jump

They cycled on for a few more minutes and there, just as the trees gave out, they came to a narrow gorge, perhaps three metres wide, with a stream raging some five metres below. The bank they were on rose up in a sort of natural ramp, and fell away on the far side.

'Drat,' said Amazon. 'I suppose we'll have to scramble down there, somehow, and then get all wet and dirty crossing the wretched thing, and then have to haul these bikes up the other side.'

Then Amazon realized that she was talking to herself.

'Time to learn how to do a real jump,' came Frazer's voice from behind her, where he had backed up along the trail. 'You'll love this. Just watch what I do, then copy it.'

Frazer began slowly, then rapidly reached full speed, and he surged up the sloping final section. At the top he sailed out and landed beautifully on the lower side of the gorge. He skidded round to face her with that infuriating grin.

'Your turn! And make sure you land evenly on both wheels.'

'B-but . . .' she began.

'Seriously, Zonnie, it's not a big deal. Because this side is lower, you can't flunk it. But, if you really want to, I'll wait here until you've climbed down, swum over and climbed up again . . .'

Amazon was a gutsy kid, but she did have one weakness: heights. And she felt doubly vulnerable, as she was going to be relying on cycling skills she wasn't sure she possessed.

It wasn't the prospect of the climb and swim combo that decided her (the stream was more of a wade than a swim, although she guessed the water would be icy cold), but the thought of chickening out of something that Frazer had done with such ease.

So, muttering various really quite bad words under her breath, she freewheeled back down the track, so she could get up enough speed for the jump.

Her legs pumped frenziedly as she ground up through the gears. A low branch brushed against her helmet, but not enough to put her off or slow her down.

The edge of the gorge came closer, closer.

She imagined herself flying.

She imagined herself falling.

Crushed and crumpled among the rocks in the stream thousands of metres below.

Amazon jammed on the brakes just a couple of metres short of the jump. It was almost a fatal mistake. The bike skidded and slid right up to the lip. The front wheel was half over the edge. Had Amazon stayed on the bike, they both would have tumbled down the gorge. As it was, she managed to nimbly leap off the bike, keeping hold of the handlebars with one hand, so that it didn't fall.

Frazer had been watching, horrified.

'You OK, Zonnie?' he cried.

'No thanks to you,' Amazon huffed back. She was a little winded, and her knee hurt, but she was basically fine.

Frazer cycled further down the trail on his side and, without pausing, made the much more difficult jump back across the gorge. He had to drag the front wheel of his bike up by sheer might and main, and even so only just made it.

'You shouldn't have come back,' said Amazon, as he helped her back on to the bike.

'The Trackers never leave a comrade behind,' he replied and, although Amazon checked for any trace of irony, she found nothing but sincerity. 'We'll climb down together. It won't be that bad.'

'Huh?' replied Amazon. She pointed to the stream coursing below them: 'Down there is the way of the wuss. I'm jumping this one.'

Frazer grinned back at her.

'I didn't doubt it for a second. We'll do it together.'

'Seriously?'

'Seriously.'

And so this time they went back together along the trail, turned and, without another word, pedalled like fury to the lip of the chasm and flew together in perfect synchrony. Their tyres hit the ground at exactly the same second.

'If only there'd been someone to film that,' said Frazer, 'it'd be a YouTube hit for sure.'

'Hmm,' said Amazon. 'Then there wouldn't be enough room in the whole of Canada for your ego.'

13

The Mountain

The going around the base of the mountain was good, and it only took them half an hour of rapid cycling to reach an area where, rather than being confronted with a near vertical wall of gunmetal-grey rock, they found a broken slope, made of fractured shale and loose boulders.

It may have been less steep than the cliff they had just bypassed, but it still looked like a pretty forbidding obstacle to Amazon. And there was something loose and shifting about the crumbly rock that she didn't at all like the look of.

'Are we really going to climb up there?' she asked. 'It looks kind of . . . unstable . . .'

'It's the highest point around. If we want to find that kid and maybe, just maybe, your parents . . .'

The thought that they might by some miracle find her parents was always there in the back of Amazon's mind.

'I know, I know. It just looks so, well, *hard.*'

'Since when were you ever afraid of hard, cuz? Heck, you've stared down big cats and bigger sharks. Not to mention –'

'OK, I get it. Where shall we stash the bikes?'

'I was thinking about that. Walking up a hill is always pretty hard work. But then so is walking down a hill – that's actually when most people fall. But *riding* down a hill . . .'

'You *are* kidding . . .?'

Frazer grinned a grin so wide that Amazon thought the top part of his head might drop off.

'OMG. You're not kidding, are you?'

'Listen, Zonnie, I've been looking for a downhill challenge like this all my life, so there's no way I'm going to leave my bike at the bottom of this hill. If you like, you can leave yours down here, but I'm pushing mine up that slope and cruising down in style. I'll wait for you back here, if that's what you want.'

Amazon looked at him, shook her head and started to push her bike up the side of the mountain.

What followed was, measured purely in terms of physical effort, the hardest two hours of Amazon Hunt's life. The slope was too steep for them to be able to push their bikes straight up, so they had to laboriously zigzag their way, traversing back and forth. Although the sky was grey and the temperature getting chilly, they were soon drenched in sweat, and both stripped down to their T-shirts, which clung clammily to their backs.

The ground itself was treacherous, and several times one or the other would lean on their bike only to find it sliding away under them on the loose gravel.

'You want to rest?' Frazer asked at one point when, although they felt like they had been travelling for hours, they seemed to have made almost no progress.

Amazon shook her head wearily. She feared that if she stopped then she'd never be able to carry on, and all the work so far would have been for nothing. So, without even pausing, she reached behind her, took the water bottle from her pack, swigged and put it back.

On they trudged, slipping and sliding, grazing their knees and barking their shins, but never pausing. More than once, their steps set off little landslides that rolled down the mountain behind them.

Soon they stopped even trying to look up at their destination, but just plodded on, heads down, like penitents on a pilgrimage to atone for untold sins.

And then Amazon did look up, more in despair than hope, and let out a shout of joy. Suddenly, in that unexpected way in which the seemingly impossible becomes real, they found that they had almost made it: the topmost ridge was just above them. They found the energy within themselves to run – well, perhaps it was more of a rapid stagger – up the final few metres. Just before the summit they found themselves on solid, jagged rock and had to leave the bikes behind, but that gave them renewed vigour. Without the weight of the bikes, they felt like spirits of the air, and leapt to the top like mountain goats, yelling with delight at each bound from boulder to boulder.

And the moment they reached the very top something miraculous happened. All the way up the skies had been a solid grey, matching almost exactly the grey of the rock. It was a joyless sky for a joyless hike. But now there was a transformation. It was as if the grey were a huge dark curtain that was suddenly thrown back, letting the glorious sun shine into a long-abandoned room.

Now the sky was a dazzling, radiant blue, made more intense by the few wispy white clouds that clung on, like the last tufts of hair on a bald man's head.

14

At the Top of the World

Amazon and Frazer stood on a flat slab of rock. Behind them was the relatively easy slope of the broken moraine field they had just ascended. In front of and below them was the great, almost vertical cliff they had skirted. The view was truly astounding. Although the mountain was modest by the standards of the Canadian Coast Range, of which it formed an outcrop, it was the highest point for many, many miles.

From up here the two Trackers could see what looked like an endless sea of trees, broken only by the upswelling islands of other mountains. The trees were mainly the same conifers through which they had cycled – Douglas firs and pine trees. However, in the valley bottoms there were patches of broadleaf trees – ash and oak – and they were now in their full riotous autumnal glory, exploding in orange and yellow and bronze. In the distance the much higher peaks of the Coast Range snapped at the sky like the teeth of a giant wolf.

Amazon and Frazer gazed around them, and then looked at each other, entirely lost for words. In theory they were there to look for the little lost boy, but Amazon was hoping she just might catch a glimpse of a campfire burning below somewhere, a fire that might lead her to her parents. But there was nothing but trees and rocks and glistening ribbons of water. There was no sign of human life, but the view was still sublime.

Finally Amazon managed to say: 'Do you think it would look this heavenly if it hadn't been such hell to get here?'

'What I think,' said Frazer, 'is that this is a heck of a good place for a picnic.'

All they ate was the trail mix and a shared chocolate bar, but it was the greatest meal either of them had ever eaten. The beauty of the setting, the ravenous hunger they had built up, and that sense that they had thoroughly earned it all combined to make each mouthful a culinary joy.

When they'd finished and stashed away their rubbish in their packs, Frazer balanced his neat little Leica camera on a pile of stones and put on the self-timer. They goofed around for a few shots. Then Frazer took some panoramic photos, covering 365 degrees.

'I'll put these up on the TRACKS Facebook page when we get back to civilization,' he said.

But those very words brought back to them what they were actually supposed to be doing.

'Right,' he continued, 'let's see what we can see.'

He took out his binoculars – a fine pair of Swarovskis that his father had given him for his eleventh birthday.

He slowly turned round, scanning the forest.

Amazon used her own sharp eyesight, gazing out again over the infinite space of the Canadian wilderness. And, as she did, her heart suddenly welled up with despair.

'This is useless,' she said, almost to herself. 'There's just . . . so much of it. How could we ever have expected to find anything? The boy . . . my parents . . . it's all so futile.'

Frazer let the binoculars hang from the leather strap round his neck.

'Amazon, if this was futile, my dad would never have begun it. He loves his brother, but more than anything he's a practical man. He never wastes his time. He plays the percentages. He's got good reasons to believe that your parents are still out there.'

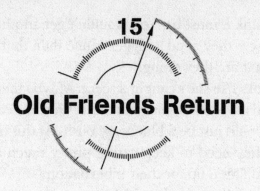

15

Old Friends Return

Amazon had been gazing into the middle distance as Frazer spoke, trying to find the hope that she knew should live in those words. But then something closer caught her eye, on the slope beneath them. Something pale. Something moving.

No, not one thing, but two.

She touched Frazer's arm.

'Look,' she said, her voice quiet, almost a whisper, despite the fact that the creatures were too far away for even a shout to reach them.

'What? Where?'

Silently, Amazon pointed down to the foot of the slope they had so recently ascended.

It was the spirit bears, mother and cub. The mother was moving warily, but also with purpose. She seemed torn between her desire to follow some scent trail and her fear of taking the cub out into the open.

'That can't really be the same two bears we saw, can it?' asked Amazon.

'I think it must be. You wouldn't get another two so close – they need a bigger range than that.'

'What are they doing?'

'Looks like she's caught a scent. Maybe there's an injured elk or something out there. Or some carrion. Or it could just be a blueberry bush. At this time of year they need to keep eating pretty much all the time to fatten up for their hibernation.'

'Have you noticed,' said Amazon, 'that she seems to be roughly following the path that we took up the slope?'

Amazon had begun that sentence without thinking through its actual meaning. But, as soon as it was out in the open, its implications were as obvious as a golden bear on a grey hillside.

Frazer gulped – Amazon thought it was perhaps a comically exaggerated gulp of the kind a nervous cartoon canary would make at the approach of a hungry cartoon cat. But it might simply have been the gulp of a boy facing up to the reality of becoming *prey*.

Still the bears came on. However, their progress was quite slow. At this rate it would take them as long as Amazon and Frazer to reach the top. Amazon asked if she could look through the binoculars. Frazer handed them over, although she could see that it took an effort of will.

'Don't drop them,' he said. 'They're top-of-the-range. They have inbuilt image stabilizers and . . .'

'Yeah, I get it,' replied Amazon.

The binoculars really were superb. It took Amazon a second or two to focus, but when she did she had to gasp. She had a visceral urge to flinch – it seemed as though the bears were literally an arm's length away.

When she had seen the bears on the lakeside, she had been so overwhelmed by both their beauty and her own fear that she had not been able to observe them in any kind of objective way. But looking at them now through the binoculars was oddly like watching them on a TV documentary. She almost imagined the narrator's voice-over:

'The Kermode bear – this rare and exquisite subspecies of the *Ursus americanus* – is chiefly at home in the dense coastal woodlands of Western Canada, and only ventures out into more open territory when the need for food drives it. Here we see the mother and her cub undertake –'

'Zonnie,' said Frazer, interrupting her daydream, 'I think maybe we should get out of here. I couldn't see any sign of any plane wreckage, or the boy. I think we should just make our way back to the campsite and wait for my dad to rejoin us.

'If we skirt down the eastern ridge of this slope, we can get back on the trail without the bears noticing us. The wind will carry our scent away from them, and unless we start singing "Yankee Doodle" the mother won't hear us. Plus, looking at it, you can see that the slope's not too bad there, even for a novice like you, so we should be able to cruise down. This is where mountain biking really gets to be fun.'

Reluctantly, Amazon agreed. She had imagined herself finding her parents and saving the kid, but now she realized that it was just a dream. She was barely more than a kid herself. It was time to admit defeat.

'Move slowly,' said Frazer, as they crept stealthily back down the slope to where they'd left the bikes. 'And keep low.'

'I thought bears couldn't see very well?' whispered Amazon.

'It's a myth. Their vision isn't as hot as their sense of smell or hearing, but they see about as well as we do. The difference is that they use all three senses when they're assessing prey, whereas we've come to rely just on vision.'

'I wish you wouldn't keep talking about us as prey,' said Amazon.

They reached the bikes without the bears noticing them. Then, as Amazon picked up her bike, her foot slipped on the loose ground. A few pebbles rolled down the slope. The pebbles set some slightly larger stones moving. And then, as Amazon and Frazer looked on, horrified, the trickle of rocks and stones rapidly snowballed, until it became a landslide. The whole hillside had been in a state of instability.

'Jeepers,' said Frazer, 'that could have happened while we were climbing up. We'd have been –'

'Frazer, look,' interrupted Amazon.

She pointed to the landslide and then at its direction. It was heading straight for the spirit bears. The mother bear seemed oblivious to the danger. She was still heading up. And then she stopped, sniffed and looked up. For a second Amazon thought that the bear was looking right at her, but later she thought that she must just have been looking towards the sound of the landslide.

'Oh no,' said Frazer, no longer bothering to keep either his voice or his body low, 'what have we done?'

It seemed both agonizingly slow and yet over in the blink of an eye. The rockfall – a mix of grit, pebbles, stones, rocks and now huge boulders – surged down the mountainside.

The mother bear turned and tried to guide her cub back towards the relative safety of the trees, but it was obvious to Amazon that they would never make it.

It seemed that the mother bear reached the same conclusion. For now she opened her great jaws and snatched up the cub. Ten metres away there was a huge boulder – too big, surely, to be carried down with the landslide, and tall enough, perhaps, to provide a refuge. The bear reached it just as the first rocks hit her. She tried to climb the boulder, but it was impossible with the heavy infant in her mouth. She just couldn't seem to scramble up. So then, using her mighty neck muscles, she hurled the clamouring cub up on to the flat top of the boulder, and then prepared to leap after it.

Too late.

The surging wall of the landslide hit her, and carried her for many metres down the slope. Her body rolled and spun in the flow, almost as if it had been water. For a few hopeful moments Amazon thought that the mother was going to be OK, that she would be able to ride out the disaster. But then she was thrown against another of the big boulders that littered the slope, and a second later another huge rock crashed into her body. Rocks piled up round her beautiful golden fur, burying her beyond hope of salvation.

For some strange reason Amazon and Frazer only registered the huge noise of the landslide because of the shocking nature of the silence that followed it. They both seemed rooted to the spot, as if lava had flowed round their feet and set them in solid rock.

There was literally not a glimpse of golden fur to be seen beneath the rubble. And now Amazon and Frazer's faces were as grey as the rocks. Tears coursed down Amazon's cheeks, and Frazer's eyes glistened.

'What have I done, what have I done?' moaned Amazon, echoing and yet subtly changing Frazer's earlier words.

'It wasn't you. It was . . . it was . . . it was just rotten luck. This whole hillside was ready to collapse at any moment. Amazon, these things happen in the wild. Animals get killed all the time.'

'But the baby . . . What can we do? We can't leave it alone out here.'

They both focused back on the little bear cub. It was still on top of the big rock. It was making the most heartbreaking sounds, a sort of sheeplike bleating, full of yearning interspersed with yelps that were both frightened and angry.

'I guess we'd better go and see if there's anything we can do,' said Frazer. 'But we can't go down that

way, and we certainly can't ride. That whole slope could go and take us with it. We can edge our way down this ridge, trying to keep to the solid rock, and then maybe work our way across when we get level with the cub.'

Amazon saw that this was a good plan. But it was one destined never to be put into operation. Through her bleary eyes, she caught another glimpse of golden fur. Not quite the perfect pale honey of the spirit bears, but lovely nevertheless. For a moment she thought that somehow the mother bear had survived the fall and shrugged off her shroud of rocks and rubble. But this new vision was too far down the slope – right at the treeline.

Another bear? Perhaps a friend of the other two? Would it adopt the cub?

Frazer now saw it too.

'Oh, jeepers,' he said, filling the silly word with dread and sorrow.

And now Amazon could see that this was no bear. No bear ever moved with that lithe, sinuous grace. No bear was ever made like this, of nothing but bone, sinew and muscle. No bear was ever quite so intent on one thing and one thing only: killing.

'Cougar,' said Amazon, even though she'd never seen a live one before.

The grace and intensity of the animal reminded her of one of the two big cats she'd seen so recently in Russia – the Amur leopard. And this cougar seemed bigger than the leopard she had come to know. Not as heavily set, perhaps, but taller and longer.

And the cougar could only be after one thing. The cub still bleated on his rock, and the puma stalked it.

16

Downhill

'That's it,' said Amazon, her eyes suddenly dry, and her face set as hard as the rock that the tiny bear stood on. 'I'm going to go and save that cub.' She clamped the helmet down on her head, picked up her bike and stood with one foot on the pedal.

'Amazon, you're nuts,' said Frazer. 'Don't you realize how dangerous a cougar is to us? It could easily kill a human. And that's without taking the chances of a landslide into account. I can't let you do this, cuz. My dad would never forgive me if –'

'You can't stop me, Frazer,' she said, shrugging off his hand. 'I thought the point of being in TRACKS was to save animals? Well, I've already killed one, and I'm not going to stand aside and watch another die. If the mother was still alive, that old cougar wouldn't dare bother the cub. I'd never forgive myself if I didn't at least try.'

And then, without giving Frazer another chance

to argue her out of it, she pushed off down the murderous slope.

Frazer, stunned, watched her go.

This was a nightmare.

It was also the chance to go for it like he'd never gone for it before. With a long-suppressed cry of '*Woo hoo!*', he kicked off after his cousin.

If Frazer enjoyed the crazy ride down the mountain, Amazon certainly did not. The long cycle through the forest didn't require any real mountain-biking skill, and even the terrifying jump over the gorge demanded more nerve than ability; but this was different. She had to use every particle of her being to keep from falling off – a fall that she knew might easily break her neck or set off another landslide that would finish her off, along with the baby bear, the cougar and probably Frazer as well.

She had to use all her natural balance to compensate for the constant sliding and skidding of the wheels; all her strength to keep the frantically bucking handlebars in line; all her intelligence to pick out the best route as she hurtled down the slope; and all of her nerve to keep the disabling waves of panic at bay.

Her eyes constantly flickered in a triangle, the three points of which were the bear, the cougar and the section of mountain right in front of her.

Twice she almost fell, but both times a well-placed

foot kept her upright, at the cost of a few more millimetres of sole worn off her trainer.

Amazon was vaguely aware of Frazer behind her. Partly it was the uncanny sixth sense that she had developed for knowing his whereabouts. But mainly it was because of his constant insane whoops and yells.

She was getting close to the big rock on which the bear cub stood. But so was the cougar, approaching it from the other side. And it was now that Amazon realized the flaw in her plan. Well, not so much a flaw as an oversight. She just hadn't given any thought as to what she should do when she reached the rock.

Would the baby bear meekly submit to her grabbing it? How could she face the cougar? And, if she did manage to somehow mount the rock, save the bear from the big cat and climb back down to her bike, how on earth was she supposed to cycle the rest of the way down carrying a bear that, although a baby, weighed as much as a sack of potatoes?

Amazon was almost at the rock now. She'd gained enough confidence as a mountain biker to make a perfect sliding stop right in front of it. She glanced back at her cousin, hoping that for once he might have done some thinking.

She saw that he had.

But it wasn't the kind of cool, rational thinking she'd been hoping for.

Bear Rescue

Frazer had, in fact, been giving serious thought to exactly these problems as he carved his way down the mountain. The fact that his brain hadn't come up with any kind of ingenious plan vaguely disappointed but didn't especially surprise him. But, all along, his body – or perhaps just a deeper, barely conscious part of his brain – knew what had to be done.

Ten metres before the rock – at about the same point that Amazon had begun to apply her brakes – Frazer performed a trick he'd done a hundred times on his old BMX, but never once on a mountain bike. He threw all his weight on to his hands, levered back and up, and got his feet on to the crossbar. He was still steering with his hands, but it was tricky – no, it was impossible – on the mountain. But he didn't need to stay like this for long. Because now it was time.

He jumped with all his might, making sure he put enough sideways pressure on the bike to send it round the rock. The rock that he was now sailing towards in mid-air.

He landed on top of it and went straight into a forward roll. But, at the same second that he leapt up on to the rock from his bike, the cougar made its leap towards the little bear too.

The cougar, intent upon its prize and partly blocked by the big rock, had failed to notice the approach of the two humans. It was therefore a little surprised to find itself sharing the rock not only with the helpless bear cub, but also with this bizarre flying human.

That surprise was the only advantage Frazer had – and he knew he only had a second. He did not pause, but carried straight on from his forward roll into a run. He stooped, picked up the little golden bear and jumped straight down from the rock. As he'd hoped, his bike had come to rest almost exactly where he landed.

'Amazon, if you want to live, get here now!' he hollered.

A moment later and she was at his side.

To her astonishment, he thrust the now squirming and protesting cub into her hands.

'Get this thing into my backpack, NOW!'

'There's no room!' she cried back.

'Dump it all.'

Behind them they heard the outraged scream of the cougar. It had been too startled to react immediately, and now it was surveying them from its vantage point up on the rock.

Humans.

It usually feared and shunned this animal. The first time it had seen one it was curious, and came to see if it was good to eat, but there had come a noise like ice cracking, and the cougar felt a pain like the snapping jaws of a wolverine, and from then on the cougar had only one ear.

And here were two of them. But these, it saw, were juveniles. Cubs, like the bear. *Its* bear. *Its* meal. *Its* prize.

Stolen.

Well, they would all pay the price.

18

Cat Chase

Somehow, Amazon managed to thrust the writhing, mewling cub into Frazer's backpack. The tight fit of the pack miraculously seemed to calm the little creature, like swaddling clothes do a human baby, and it instantly settled into the pack, with just its nose resting on Frazer's shoulder. It would have been rather a pleasant sensation had Frazer not known that something infinitely sharper and more deadly than the cub's wet nose might soon be sinking into the back of his neck.

Amazon looked back towards the screaming cougar, and saw it properly for the first time. She knew enough about animals to be very aware of the fact that it makes no sense to think of any animal – even a cunning and powerful predator such as the cougar – as evil. Evolution has shaped all animals to be efficient at obtaining nutrition, at evading predators, at passing on their genes. Animals were incapable of malice, of cruelty, of vengeance. These were all human failings.

But, as well as being a naturalist, she was also a thirteen-year-old girl, and what she saw before her terrified her. The snarling mouth seemed to betray a boundless appetite for death. The superbly lithe form had the grace of a samurai sword, made for dealing death.

And it was getting ready to spring at her now.

'Frazer, we've got to –'

'GO!' he yelled, and four wheels spun on the loose gravel; spun and then gripped. Not a second too soon. The cougar landed in their tracks. The small stones thrown up by the spinning tyres momentarily blinded the cat, and the pause generated was enough to give the Trackers a few metres' head start. But then the cougar bounded forward again, each long-legged leap covering three metres. It ate up the ground between it and the frantically careering bikes.

Amazon and Frazer could hear the paws striking the ground just behind them. Hear, even, the hot breath of their pursuer. Only the bear cub seemed oblivious to the danger. He had been walking all day, and the swaddled security of the bag had lulled him into a stupor.

The one advantage Amazon and Frazer had was that they were heading downhill. Most animals would much rather run on the flat – or even uphill – than down. Mountain bikes, however, more than any other form of transportation ever devised by humankind, were made to go *down*.

Instinctively, Amazon and Frazer stayed close together, carving left and right in unspoken harmony. But no matter how quickly they went, and no matter how handicapped the cougar was by the awkwardness of bounding downhill, it was still gaining on them.

Right in front of Amazon and Frazer rose another huge rock. Frazer was on the left, and so naturally broke that way. Amazon went to the right.

The mountain lion was briefly confused by the split, undecided about which way to go. In its confusion, the cougar's front feet slid, then caught in the ground, and the animal half somersaulted into the rock. It was badly winded, but not seriously hurt. And now it was madder than ever.

Amazon and Frazer met again on the far side of the boulder. Without knowing exactly what had happened behind them, they sensed that they had gained some time.

They were now only fifty metres from the treeline. However, the trees represented anything but safety. They had been just about able to hold their own cycling downhill on the open mountainside, but in the forest they would hardly be able to cycle at all, and the cat would be in its element.

Then Frazer saw what he had been looking for: the rough trail that they had taken round from the cliff side of the mountain continued on. It would lead them away from the route back to the campsite, but, he reasoned, that was something they could put right later on. Staying alive, not getting back, was the pressing issue.

'Head for that trail,' he yelled, and pointed at the gap in the dense line of trees.

Just before they entered the dark of the forest, Amazon looked back over her shoulder. And there, a streak of dark gold against the grey slate, she saw the cougar giving chase.

19

Into the Trees

The trail was similar to the one they had taken to reach Mount Humboldt: well-worn earth, generally flat, with a few small rises and undulations. In other words it was a perfect cross-country bike ride. Or it would have been had they not had North America's most dangerous predator on their tail.

They were going in single file now. Frazer had ushered Amazon ahead, saying, 'You first, Zonnie – that way I know I haven't left you behind.'

Another time, Amazon would have stopped to argue the point, but she told herself she'd get him for it later. Except that she wouldn't be getting him, because she knew that for once he was talking good sense. It also meant that he was the one who would be in the most danger. The fear of putting Frazer in peril made Amazon pedal even faster than she would have done had it been her own life at stake. And it wasn't just for Frazer: there was the precious cargo he carried – the orphaned cub.

And so they flew through the forest. She took jumps without even thinking. By the third one she was able to marry technique with courage, and she heard Frazer's shouts of encouragement gradually give way to whoops of admiration.

She looked back a couple of times. Frazer thought she was checking on him, but she was really looking beyond him along the trail for their hunter. And she saw nothing.

But then there came a subtle change. Each rise now seemed a little longer than the subsequent fall. And the flat sections were no longer quite flat, but inclined slightly upwards. They were climbing. It was slow and undramatic, and had they been walking they would hardly have noticed. But on a bike it was different. The little moments of rest provided by the down sections were gone. Now every metre forward had to be bought with effort.

Sweat began to pour down Amazon's face, stinging her eyes. She wiped them with her sleeve, hit a root and almost fell.

'Careful, cuz!' shouted Frazer from behind.

She was too tired to shout back.

And the worst thing was she didn't know how long this would continue for. Most big cats, unlike the hunters of the dog family, don't have the stamina for a long chase like this. A lion or leopard would have given up long ago, after its first rush was thwarted. But Amazon just didn't know enough about the cougar to figure out if it was the same.

Just as Amazon was reaching the end of her ability to go on, she noticed that the ground on the right-hand side of the trail had fallen away. Looking over, she saw a ribbon of white water tumbling below. Was this the same river they had jumped earlier, or just another springing from the same mountain source? She didn't know, didn't really care, but the sound and sight – perhaps even the smell of the water – reminded her that she was desperately thirsty. She had never been this thirsty in her life – not even on the remote desert island she and Frazer had been marooned on not long before.

She couldn't go on.

She had to drink.

At the top of the next rise, she stopped and reached for her water bottle. There was a bare mouthful left. She tore off the top and gulped it down. So perfect, so cool. But so little of it. Frazer pulled up next to her.

'We can't . . .'

'I know we can't, but I was going to DIE!'

'OK, I get it,' said Frazer soothingly. 'Anyway, I think maybe we shook that thing off. I don't reckon it had ever come across two mountain bikers of our quality before. I –'

It was then that the cougar leapt. And this time there was no sound. The whole concentrated energy of the beast went into this killing leap, with nothing left over for anything as superfluous as a snarl.

20

Headless

Frazer and Amazon, standing astride their bikes, were close together. But the cougar had only one target in mind. It was going for the smaller and weaker of the two animals.

Like other feline hunters, the cougar has two main killing techniques: the suffocating throat hold and the crunching bite through the spinal column. The former would be used to kill the bigger prey: white-tailed deer and elk, and even the odd moose. It could take many minutes to kill an animal like that, and it could be dangerous for the hunter. A struggling elk could easily kill a cougar with the point of an antler. The latter – the single savage bite slicing through the backbone – would be used for smaller prey. The cat regarded Amazon Hunt as small enough to be dispatched with a single bite.

She never even saw the leap. The cougar had tracked them along the side of the path, silent and invisible.

She did not see it, but she did feel it. Felt the lunging, shadowy doom of it.

And so she ducked. No, it wasn't anything as conscious as ducking. It was a flinch.

It was not sufficient to make the cat miss its victim, but it did miss its precise target. Rather than the nape of the neck, the iron jaws and five-centimetre canines closed round the head.

The hard, shiny, hairless head.

Which promptly fell off.

Had Amazon not snapped open the chinstrap on her helmet, the cougar would have taken her down with it. The cat, clinging with tooth and claw to the helmet, flew over her, and crashed down the slope, rolling and tumbling until it reached the turbulent waters below.

The two Trackers did not wait to see what became of it. Propelled now by a new lease of terror-pumped adrenalin, they cycled. They could hardly have gone more quickly had rocket engines been attached to their bikes. They reached the top of the long, low hill they'd been hauling themselves up, and then zoomed down the long slope on the far side of it. As they cycled, they grew sure that this time they'd left the horror behind them.

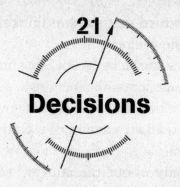

21

Decisions

Amazon and Frazer climbed off their bikes and sat on the trunk of a fallen pine. The bear cub was still fast asleep in the rucksack. Amazon took the pack carefully from Frazer's back, and cuddled it and the bear on her knee. It looked more like a toy than a real, flesh-and-blood animal.

The forest around them was dark and almost silent. It was growing much cooler, and the sweat from the hard ride felt cold on their backs. Spiders' webs as big as cartwheels glimmered and shivered in the failing light. A few insects buzzed around, but it was too late in the season for the clouds of mosquitoes or blackfly or the other biting pests that can make life hell in the Canadian forests in summer.

'How you doing, Zonnie?' Frazer asked, looking at his cousin with some concern. Her face was blotched with red from the effort, but beneath it she was white and trembling. And her eyes brimmed with tears that she would not let fall.

Frazer assumed that she was thinking about her brush with the cougar.

'That was some lucky escape,' he said, smiling. 'If you hadn't undone your helmet strap . . . well, maybe we could have beaten the cat off, but it wouldn't have been easy. I read an account of a cougar attack on a family –'

'I don't care about the cougar,' said Amazon tragically. 'I've just killed a mother bear. I've made an orphan of this little one.' Finally, now, the tears began to flow. 'What can we do with it?' she sobbed.

In the relatively short time they'd been hanging out together Frazer had never seen Amazon cry before. In fact, if anyone had asked him, he'd have said that nothing could make Amazon Hunt cry. Well, perhaps he should have known that nothing could make Amazon cry for *herself*. She was sobbing not for her own misfortunes, but for the little creature in their care, and for the harm – albeit accidental – she, or rather they, had caused.

Frazer put his arm round her.

'Zonnie, maybe you haven't noticed it, but you work for one of the best-resourced animal welfare organizations on the planet. We have links to every responsible zoo and wildlife park in the world. And back on the farm in New England we have plenty of room for a bear. So don't worry about Goldilocks here. We'll find the right home for her.'

Amazon couldn't help but smile through her tears.

'Goldilocks?'

'Well, yeah, I know Goldilocks wasn't technically a bear, but she hung out with bears. And, well, this little girl does have mighty pretty blonde hair.'

Amazon's smile grew, and then faded again.

'All you mentioned were zoos . . . Is there no way we could give Goldilocks to another mother bear, so she could grow up in the wild?'

Frazer shook his head.

'I don't think so. An adult bear that wasn't this one's biological mother would probably kill it. The best we could do is to give her a safe home, and maybe let her take part in a captive breeding programme – you heard my dad say how rare these spirit bears are.'

Amazon's head slumped, but then she sat up straight again.

'Fine. I can't bring back the mother from the dead, but we can bring this little bear back to safety. Now which way is the camp?'

A shadow crossed Frazer's face. 'Ah,' he said, 'that might be a bit of a problem.'

'Don't tell me . . . your pack . . . the stuff I emptied out . . .'

'Exactly. I didn't have time to chew it over. But the map and my compass were in there.'

'But we still have these,' said Amazon, holding up her GPS watch.

'Yep, we do, and that'll tell us our position, but it

won't mean much without a map. But you're right, there's a compass function, and I think I know roughly what direction we need to head in. Trouble is, though . . .'

'Yeah?'

'Well, it's getting late. It took us three hours to reach the mountain. Then we've come quite a distance further on. Not sure how far, but we were cycling at top speed for an hour. And the trails through these forests are pretty good as long as you're travelling in daylight and can see where you're going . . .'

The startling reality of the situation dawned on Amazon.

'Are you saying it's too late to get back tonight?'

'Afraid so, Zonnie. The best thing we can do is to find a campsite, build a fire and hunker down till morning.'

Amazon Hunt thought about the cougar, then about the little bear. And then, as the first howl echoed over the wide forest, she thought about the wolves.

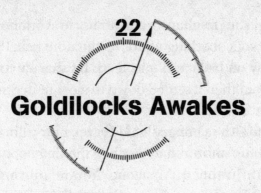

22

Goldilocks Awakes

Amazon had always loved the idea of wolves, but that howl, even though it sounded very far away, made the hair on the back of her neck stand up. And of course there was Hal Hunt's harrowing story about his and her father's encounter, all those years before.

However, before she had the chance to put her fear into words, Goldilocks woke up. Woke up and realized that she was not happy. She began to struggle wildly within the tight confines of Frazer's backpack, emitting a stream of grumbles, yelps, wails, moans and growls.

Strangely, this was exactly what Amazon needed. She had an almost magical way with animals, a sort of natural empathy that meant that dogs and cats would come to her unbidden, birds would lie quietly in her hands while she put a splint on a broken leg or wing, and that made foxes and badgers play happily with their young, even though she was only a couple of metres away.

And she put that special ability to work now. She spoke soft, soothing words to the little bear. She let it chew on her hand – its teeth bit sharply to begin with, but then it settled down to a contented sucking on her thumb.

'Guess she's hungry,' said Frazer, marvelling at the way that Amazon had soothed the tiny cub.

'Duh!' replied Amazon. 'You're missing your mother's milk, aren't you, little girl?'

And the thought of that almost brought on another bout of silent weeping.

'Try some trail mix on her,' suggested Frazer. 'She's old enough to be eating solid food as well as drinking milk.'

Amazon sprinkled the seeds and nuts on her hand and presented them to the inquisitive nose. Goldilocks snuffled the mix of dried fruit and nuts, and then gobbled it up greedily. Two more handfuls went the same way.

'Well,' said Frazer, looking on, 'I guess that *we* can eat worms and bark tonight. But we should find a better place to camp before it's dark.'

Goldilocks, calm and contented now, was stashed back in Amazon's rucksack, and they climbed back on the bikes.

'What exactly are we looking for?' asked Amazon. She hadn't done much camping, so she had to rely on Frazer's expert knowledge.

'Water, that's the main thing. Of course we need

shelter as well, but I can easily improvise something from branches. I've brought a little friend with me from the South Seas to help out.'

'What, a coconut?'

'Ha ha.'

Then Frazer reached into a side pocket on his backpack and pulled out a long, straight-bladed machete. It gleamed evilly in the fading light. And, as ever when he pulled out his machete, he couldn't stop himself from making a *shwiiiiiinnnng* noise, as though he were a knight or a samurai warrior in a movie. And, as usual, Amazon laughed at him for it.

But she was also mightily relieved to see the formidable blade.

'How do we find water? I don't fancy going back and sharing it with that cougar . . .'

'Zonnie, we're in Canada, not the Gobi Desert. If we carry on, the water will find us.'

And sure enough, after another fifteen minutes of cycling, they came to a stream that crossed their trail.

'Will this do?' asked Amazon. 'I mean, it's getting late . . .'

She was right – the afternoon was fading fast into evening. And it was getting colder.

Frazer looked around at the dense wall of trees and tangled undergrowth.

'Well, it's water, but there's nowhere to camp here. Let's see if we can follow the stream. In Canada water likes company.'

'You mean leave the trail? Is that wise?' asked Amazon. 'What if we get lost . . .? At least here we know roughly how to retrace our steps.'

'Hey, relax, if this doesn't work out, we can just backtrack along the stream.'

They had to dismount to follow the stream on foot, pushing their bikes along with them. The going was tough and they were constantly snagged by overhead branches and patches of briars and brambles. But soon the stream was joined by another flowing down from the high ground around them.

'Here?' asked Amazon hopefully. The bear on her back was getting heavier by the second, and she was desperate to lay down her burden.

Frazer looked round, shook his head and forged on, using the mountain bike as a battering ram to force his way through the undergrowth.

And then, after twenty minutes of hard slog, they saw the forest open up before them.

'Exactly what I was hoping for,' said Frazer.

23

Beaver Lake

It was a lake – about as wide as a good stone's throw, and three or four times that in length. All around it the trees had been cut back, leaving the banks clear and flat.

Frazer nodded to himself. It was the perfect place to camp.

'You see down the far end?' he said, pointing along the length of the lake.

Amazon looked and saw an untidy barrier of sticks and mud.

Although she had never seen one before, she knew instantly what it must be.

'Beavers!'

'Yep, that's it. The beavers made this lake by damming the stream we've been following. And you see that mound over there –' Frazer pointed to a bank of mud swelling up from the water about five metres from the dam – 'that's the lodge where they live. The entrance is under the water so they're completely safe from predators. They really are very clever animals. The lake creates the perfect environment for new saplings to grow up – which is exactly what they eat.'

'They eat trees?'

'Not the whole tree, just the layer directly inside the bark. But, apart from people, no other mammal creates their own environment like this. They are the great engineers of the animal world.'

'Talking of making your own environment,' said Amazon, 'how about we do something to improve our own? It's getting cold and Goldilocks and I would appreciate a fire.'

'I'm on it!' said Frazer. 'You wait here with Goldilocks and I'll get wood and kindling.'

Frazer consciously fought the temptation to go *shwiiiiiinnnng* when he took the machete out of his pack.

He disappeared into the trees, leaving Amazon alone with Goldilocks. The bear woke up briefly, looked around, saw Amazon, made a contented little grunt and went back to sleep.

'Hard work being a baby bear, eh?' smiled Amazon. She was more determined than ever to bring the cub to safety.

Sitting by the lonely lakeside, Amazon began to get a little jumpy. She half imagined yellow eyes peering at her from the trees. A bird gave an alarm call and then flew clumsily through the branches.

The noise startled her, and the relief that followed from her realization that it was nothing more than a pigeon was in its turn followed by a shiver of apprehension about what had alarmed the bird.

'Frazer, is that you?' she called into the darkness.

There was no reply.

And then, drifting faintly through the forest, she heard, for the second time, the long, haunting cry of a wolf.

If anything, the wolf howl was further away than when Amazon had heard it on the trail. But then she had been with Frazer, and now she was alone.

'Frazer . . .?' she called again. It was now dark enough for the trees to blend together: no longer individual trunks and branches, they were now just that mysterious collective entity, The Forest.

As a child, her parents had taught her that the traditional fairy-tale terrors were imaginary. That there were no ogres or witches, and that wolves – the first and deadliest of the fairy-tale animals – were almost never a threat to humans. But that knowledge did not seem to help her now, here in a very real forest. And somehow the fact that wolves were here meant that those other long-banished nightmare figures might also be out there. So, if the wolves did not eat her, then the witch or the ogre might.

And that train of thought took Amazon back to her parents again, and she longed to have them here, protecting her.

She had been staring with all her might into the forest when she suddenly had the strongest feeling that she herself was being watched. And yet it did not feel to her that the watcher was out there, among the trees.

The hairs stood up on the back of her neck. And then she heard it.

An almost gentle, infinitely stealthy sound.

From behind her.

In the water.

Whatever was watching her had approached from the lake. Amazon spun round, expecting to see the cougar there, ready to spring from the shallows. She was getting ready to make herself seem bigger, standing on tiptoes and holding out her arms – a trick she'd read about. She was going to scream, and possibly even run at the beast – do everything to

make it clear to the cougar that she was not any predator's idea of easy pickings.

And then she saw it. Or rather them. Two long brown snouts low in the water, and four beady brown eyes staring at her in the dying light.

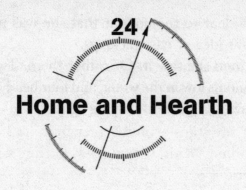

24

Home and Hearth

'You know, some outdoorsy types are more afraid of beavers than they are of bears.'

Now Amazon did scream. She had been so focused on whatever it was out there on the lake that she hadn't heard her cousin return.

The scream made the two heads – belonging to the pair of beavers who had created this lake, and very much felt that they owned it and that anyone who wanted to camp there should really ask their permission – dip below the tranquil surface of the water.

'Frazer!' yelled Amazon. 'Don't sneak up on people like that. It frightened Goldilocks.'

The little bear was still fast asleep.

'Yeah, so I see,' said Frazer. He had his arms full of pine branches, and there were four good logs, as thick as a leg, on the ground where he'd dumped them.

'Right, two jobs. Fire and shelter. Fire first. Let's

get this thing started before it's too dark to see what we're doing.'

Amazon watched carefully as Frazer made the fire. She'd seen him do it before, but it was still fascinating. Something about the almost sacred process of creating fire transformed Frazer from a kid into a man – or maybe just from a goofy kid into a slightly more serious one.

He began by arranging the four long pine logs into a cross shape, with a small gap in the middle.

That was new to Amazon, but she waited to see what Frazer would do before asking him about it. He piled smaller sticks and stouter pieces of wood into the space between the big logs. Then he used his machete to trim the bark from more pine branches. Next he cut into the exposed white wood without severing it from the branch, creating a feathery effect.

The next stage Amazon had seen before. Frazer took some strips of silver-birch bark from his pocket and used his knife to scrape at the inside lining of the bark, forming a fluffy white mass of curled shavings. He arranged this on a bed of more birch bark and small dry twigs.

'Now the fun part. You want to do this?'

Frazer held out the pencil-shaped rod of dull metal – his firesteel – and his hunting knife towards Amazon. She'd watched him use the firesteel before, in the Russian Far East, but had never had a go herself. She took the implements from Frazer.

'Remember to use the back of the knife, not the sharp part of the blade,' he said. 'And try not to cut your finger off. I could probably sew it back on with a fishbone needle and some thread made from willow bark, but my stitches are never very neat, and I might sew it on the wrong way round or something, so you'll never be able to pick your nose or scratch your butt properly again.'

Amazon wrinkled her nose in disdain. Then, concentrating, she scraped the blunt edge of the knife along the length of the metal rod. A cascade of sparks spilled out on to the birch tinder, where they crackled and fizzed, and soon set the oil-rich bark alight. Then Frazer used the little fire to set the feathered pine branches alight. They burned beautifully with a thick oily orange flame, and it was then an easy job to get the larger pile of bark and sticks in the space at the centre of the cross made by the pine logs to catch. Together they built the fire up round the burning heart.

'Nice work, Zonnie,' said Frazer admiringly, once they saw that their fire was going strongly. 'It took me about a year to get all that right. But now for the final masterstroke. You see these four branches?' he said, pointing at the logs arranged in a cross. 'Well, all we have to do to keep the fire going is to push them in towards the centre of the fire – no traipsing out into the forest for more wood. Should keep us going all night.'

'Yeah, clever,' said Amazon. 'But doesn't that mean that we'll have to stay awake so we can push the logs in?'

'Erm, well, yes, I suppose technically you do sort of, but . . . well, you could do that without even getting out of your sleeping bag.'

'Hmmm,' replied Amazon thoughtfully. 'You mean the sleeping bags we don't have?'

'Ah yes,' continued Frazer, as if this were all part of his brilliant plan. 'I designed our shelter around that very fact. We need something to keep the rain – or snow – off our heads, and our bodies dry and away from the cold, wet ground. Combined with the fire, you won't miss your sleeping bag.'

For the next ten minutes Frazer busied himself with the machete. He cut two stout branches, as long as his outstretched arms, each with a Y-shaped fork at the top. He used the machete to bore a couple of holes in the ground, and then hammered the stakes into them, using a stone from the lake. Then he angled two more sticks from the ground to the Y-joint. He used his knife to cut long strips of willow bark and lashed the upright and the diagonal poles together.

That part made Amazon smile – she knew very well that Frazer always had string in his pockets the way other people carried hankies or money, but he just had to prove that he could do without it.

Next he laid a thick layer of spruce branches over

the stakes, forming a lean-to shelter, open on one side.

'You are such a copycat,' Amazon said to him. 'You totally stole that from Makha and Dersu.'

Makha and Dersu were members of the Udege tribe in the Russian Far East. They had helped the Trackers on their mission to save the endangered Amur leopards.

'Amazon,' said Frazer, his face serious to the point of being pompous, 'among us explorers and, er, wilderness types, there is no "mine" or "yours", only "ours". You can't "steal" an idea like this; all you can do is share it. But this isn't finished yet. I told my dad about the shelter the Udege guys made, and he said it would be even better with a little addition.'

Then Frazer carried on working. He used the machete to trim more pine branches, two about the same length as the shelter, two about the same width. This time he lashed them together using thin roots from the pines, prised from the ground with his versatile machete. The poles formed a square frame the size of a single bed. Frazer then lashed more poles across the frame. Finally he put fresh green branches of spruce across the bed, piling them up thickly.

Throughout it all Amazon had helped by holding bits of wood while he bound them together, or by collecting the spruce branches. He'd done his best to make her feel as if she were a partner in the creation of their shelter. But now she stood back and said, 'OK, Frazer, I hand it to you. This is a pretty good little house you've built here.'

Frazer guessed that there would be a sting in the tail. There was.

'A pretty good house for *one*, that is. Or are we all supposed to squeeze in there?'

'It's the only way to keep warm,' replied Frazer, looking just as unhappy with the situation as Amazon. 'We can keep Goldilocks in the middle to act as a living hot-water bottle. But seriously, Zonnie, even with the fire it's going to get cold tonight, real cold, so desperate measures are called for. Right, let's see about supper.'

They emptied their packs to see what they had left. As well as a few handfuls of trail mix, they had four protein bars, two bars of chocolate and the packet soup.

Frazer tried to put on a brave face. 'We've got fire, we've got shelter, we've got food, sorta, and we've got water. That's a recipe for three happy campers.'

There was a tin cup in Amazon's pack. She filled it with lake water. She was thirsty now, despite the cold, but Frazer warned her against drinking the water straight from the lake.

She looked sceptical, saying, 'But surely there's no pollution out here? We're in the middle of nowhere.'

'Beaver fever,' he said ominously.

'Huh?'

'It's a bacterial disease you can get from drinking lake water. It's carried in beavers', ah, urine . . .'

'*Eew!*'

'The chances are we'd be OK, but it's probably best to boil it.'

Frazer rigged up a tripod arrangement with three sticks, and dangled the cup over the flames, putting that string of his to good use. They used the boiled water to make up the soup, and then boiled some more to fill up their water bottles.

With the fire burning brightly and some food inside them, Amazon and Frazer both felt a little more cheerful. It helped that they hadn't heard any more of the wolves.

Goldilocks had emerged from her slumbers by this stage. She ate everything they put in front of her, which cemented the love between the bear and the two Trackers. But her real bond was with Amazon.

'Looks like she sees you as her mother now,' said Frazer, as the bear snuggled down in Amazon's lap. 'We'll cycle out of here tomorrow and be back at the camp by tomorrow afternoon. My dad'll give us some serious grief about this, but when he sees the spirit bear we've rescued he'll forgive us everything.'

And then, as if to show up Frazer's words as nothing but hollow optimism, they heard the howling of a wolf. And this time it was closer. And a moment later it was joined by other wolves, their voices filling the night sky with banshee wails.

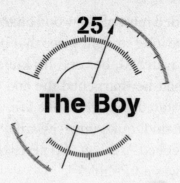

25

The Boy

The bear cub on Amazon's lap pricked up its ears, and then squirmed even further into her midriff, as if it were trying to lose itself entirely in her.

Frazer stood up and approached the treeline.

'What are you doing?' Amazon hissed. 'Come back by the fire.'

'They're a long way off still,' Frazer replied. 'And we need more wood.'

He went into the forest again, and Amazon heard the swish and hack of the machete.

'It's a bit green,' he said, when he came back, 'but I think we need to build the fire up as much as we can.'

Seeing Frazer take the wolf situation seriously was both a relief and a shock to Amazon. She'd secretly hoped that he would laugh at the wolf threat, thereby showing it to be a figment of her imagination.

Well, clearly he wasn't laughing. But having him calm and resolute in the face of this new danger was a comfort. Of sorts.

Frazer loaded most of the wood on to the fire. But there was one long straight piece that he held back. As Amazon watched, he used his knife to strip off the bark. Then he sharpened the end of the stick, and finally rotated it slowly in the fire.

'Spear,' he said, quite unnecessarily.

'Really?' replied Amazon. 'I'd never have guessed. I thought it was a toothpick.'

That made them both laugh, which broke the tension. But then something caught their attention, silencing them again.

It was Goldilocks that heard it first, pricking her ears: the unmistakable sound of something moving through the undergrowth. Frazer gave Amazon the machete, put his knife in his belt, took his spear and stood in front of the fire. In the flickering firelight he looked strangely timeless to Amazon. Standing there with the spear and the knife, he wasn't a modern boy from Long Island any more, but a Native American brave, or an Ancient Greek, or an aboriginal hunter.

And then a second noise was added to the sound of the creature moving heavily through the forest. And it was a sound that made Amazon's blood run cold. It was a high, haunting, heartbreaking sound. It did not sound to Amazon like any living creature, any animal that she had ever seen or heard or read about. She had been stalked by killer bears and tigers in Siberia, and hunted by sharks in Polynesia, but she had experienced nothing like this. It seemed not to belong to the realm of nature at all. It was the sound of a soul in torment, a ghost, or a ghoul.

As she looked, she saw the courageous and resolute Frazer first take a step back and then retreat behind the fire, putting its flames between him and whatever wretched, bloodsucking, soul-stealing being it was that was approaching them.

And then the high keening sound became clearer and they heard it for what it was.

'I WANT MY MOMMY!'

26

The Lost Boy

'What the . . .?'

Frazer and Amazon exchanged baffled glances, and then looked back to where the voice was coming from. A moment later, a tiny figure stepped – or rather staggered – into the circle of flickering light cast by the fire.

It was a child – a little boy of perhaps six years old. His blond hair was matted and filthy, his face smudged with dirt and tears, and his clothes hung from him in shreds. He was wearing a single shoe.

They both knew straight away who it was.

'Ben?' said Amazon, rushing towards him. 'Ben Waits?'

The little boy's face was filled with emotions too complex to read – certainly too complex to belong in the face of a child so young. There was hope and fear and, the topmost layer, a sort of anger or outrage. It was an expression that screamed out the child's sense of injustice, that overpowering feeling that something had happened that *just wasn't fair*.

'You're not my mommy! Where's my mommy?'

Without another word, Amazon swept the little boy, who was, indeed, the lost Ben Waits, into her arms and hugged him.

The child fought against her for a few seconds, kicking out with his one good foot, and pummelling Amazon's back with his tiny fists. But then he subsided into heart-rending sobs, as Amazon comforted him.

'We're going to take you to your mummy,' she said. 'You'll see her soon. And your daddy.'

'You talk funny,' said the little boy. 'You say "mommy" all wrong.'

'Tell me about it, kid,' said Frazer. 'She's from some rainy little island next door to Europe, where they haven't learned to speak proper American. Now come on, little guy, and get warm by the fire.'

They sat on the platform that Frazer had made, and gave Ben some trail mix and a chocolate bar, which he ate first with suspicion and then in a frenzy.

The child was clearly traumatized. He wouldn't let go of Amazon as he munched. She tried to ask him about where he'd been, and what had happened to him, but he would not answer. In fact, he seemed unable to even hear what she was saying.

They had almost forgotten about Goldilocks, but the baby bear woke at the smell of the chocolate. She was still trapped in the tight embrace of the backpack, but she squirmed and snuffled and grumbled, and made her presence felt and heard.

Ben looked up and saw the cub, ghost-pale in the dim light. The effect on him was instant. He went rigid with fear, and then tried to scramble away.

Frazer grabbed him. At the same moment he realized what must be going through the little boy's mind – the report had said that his party had been attacked by a spirit bear. The sight of even this tiny specimen had brought back what must be terrible memories.

'Hey, it's OK, little man. This is just a baby we're looking after. He's on his own as well, like you.'

Ben appeared to calm down a fraction, but still he stared intently at the bear cub as Amazon let her lick at the smears of chocolate on the wrapper. Her antics were so cute and amusing that the boy's look soon softened, and the first hint of a smile tugged at the corners of his mouth.

'Do you want to hold her?' asked Amazon, thinking that it might help to cure his fear.

Ben shook his head, and was about to say, 'Nah.' But the decision was taken out of his hands, as Goldilocks finally escaped from her prison, and jumped into the boy's arms. After a second of shocked silence, Ben exploded into giggles.

'Hey, I've got my own real-life teddy bear,' he said. 'I'm so lucky. Wait till I tell them at school. They'll think I'm making it up, so you'll have to tell them that it's true. Can I have him to keep? What's his name? Why is he whitey-yellowy? Is he a real bear? Where's his mommy?'

'She's a girl and she's called Goldilocks,' said Frazer. 'We're just looking after her for a while. We're going to take you both back where you'll be safe.'

Frazer and Amazon looked at each other, and then at the two newest members of this particular TRACKS expedition, who were now rolling around together on the floor of the platform. Amazon wondered if this feeling within her of protectiveness and pride might be what her parents felt – heck, what all parents feel – for their child.

Frazer was just about to say that it was time to settle down to get some sleep, when another voice interrupted. A voice that sent a chill through them all, from the little bear on up.

It was the long, slow howling of a wolf.

27

Bedtime

The bear and the boy scooted round in between Frazer and Amazon on the platform, with the flames of the fire in between them and the wolf howl, as if the flames could burn away the terror of that spectral voice.

But then that one wolf howl was joined by another, and then another, until the whole forest seemed to resound and echo with their voices, like a great organ in a cathedral.

Frazer spoke to Amazon in a tense whisper.

'You stay back here in the shelter,' he said. 'It's not much, but it'll give you some protection.'

'What? Where the heck are you going?'

'Keep your hair on. I'm just going to use some of the wood I collected earlier to set up perimeter fires. We want to keep them as far away as possible.'

'But they wouldn't really attack us, would they? The story your dad told us about his father . . . I mean, he said it was incredibly uncommon for wolves to attack people . . .?

'It is uncommon. But now we've got both a young child with us and a baby bear. Bears and wolves don't get on. Bears kill wolves when they can, and wolves will kill and eat bear cubs if they come across them undefended.'

'Well,' said Amazon, determination making her stick her jaw out, 'this bear cub is definitely defended!'

'I hear you, Zonnie. But we've also got Ben to look after. Wolves are afraid of adult humans, but kids . . . well, we're definitely on the menu.' Then he leaned forward and plucked a stick from the fire. 'Luckily we've got humanity's oldest friend right here, and it's time to call in a favour.'

'At least take your silly spear,' said Amazon, her harsh words failing to conceal the concern in her voice. She held out the short spear. It was surprisingly weighty and solid. Even holding it made her feel a little more secure.

But Frazer shook his head.

'You keep it for now. The wolves are still miles off. And I've got work to do.'

Amazon retreated right back into the lean-to shelter with Ben and Goldilocks while Frazer quickly built up a ring of smaller fires round their encampment. It didn't take long, as he had already dragged in plenty of wood, and he could easily get the fires going using logs from the first fire, which was still burning brightly in front of the shelter.

Frazer looked at his handiwork and nodded.

'They'll burn out before morning,' he said, half to Amazon, half to himself, 'but it may still be enough . . .'

He went to crouch beside Amazon in the shelter. Ben and Goldilocks, both exhausted, had already fallen asleep.

'You get some shut-eye too,' said Frazer. 'I'll wake you in a couple of hours.'

But it wasn't Frazer who woke Amazon. It wasn't Frazer because he was himself fast asleep, nestled next to her in the thick bed of pine branches. And nor, although the fire had died down to embers and she was shivering, was it the cold that interrupted her dreams.

It was the low, urgent growling.

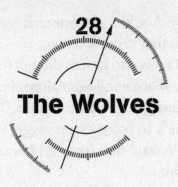

28

The Wolves

She opened her eyes and saw what she had dreaded. A dark shape was edging towards them, barely visible in the light from the sickle moon and the scattered stars. But the fact that Amazon could only just make it out didn't change the fact that there was only one thing that this could be. She tugged at Frazer's sleeve.

'*Whaaa?*' said her cousin groggily.

'They're here,' she hissed. 'The wolves.'

It normally took endless minutes of nagging and shoving to get Frazer out of bed, but now, like Amazon, he was wide awake in a second.

'Where?' he said. 'How many?'

Amazon pointed into the gloom. 'There. I don't know how many. I think I only saw one. But it's hard to tell.'

Frazer sprang up, and reached for the spear he had placed just inside their shelter. He knew that, like most predators, the wolves responded instinctively to animal behaviour: act like prey and they treated you like prey. Act like you yourself were a vicious predator and they'd think again.

And yes, it looked to him as though there was only one of them. Wolves will hunt alone, but not usually against anything larger than a hare. They needed the whole pack to bring down bigger animals, and Frazer had decided that tonight he was going to be the bigger animal.

So he dashed towards the dark shadow, yelling out a war cry and thrusting with his home-made spear. And, as he lunged forward, he also kicked at one of the logs protruding from the fire, sending up a shower of sparks. The wolf – a lean and hungry-looking male – snarled and snapped, but then cringed back from the onslaught, slinking into the night.

'Help me get this fire going again,' said Frazer over his shoulder to Amazon. 'He'll be back soon enough with the rest of the pack.'

He was talking bravely – and had acted with courage – but Frazer was frightened. Their only hope was the fire. He quickly worked at building it up, pushing the four logs together, and piling more wood on top. He used pine cones to help get it going. They burned brightly, but not for long. He used his machete to trim two more pine branches, each as thick as a broom handle.

He looked back and saw Amazon encircling Ben with one arm and the baby bear with the other.

'I'm going to need you out here, when they come

back,' he said. 'We've got to show the wolves that we're not afraid.'

'But these two . . .' protested Amazon, signalling helplessly with her hands.

'Ben,' said Frazer, looking into the boy's wide eyes, 'I'm going to need you to do a very important job. You have to look after Goldilocks for us. She's only a baby bear, and she'll need someone to cuddle her while we scare these silly wolves off.'

'I'm not afraid of wolves,' said Ben, sticking out his chin. 'I'll bash them if they try to hurt my bear.'

'I know you will!' said Frazer, grinning despite the desperate situation.

Amazon arrived at his side. She looked at her watch.

'It's four a.m. What time does it get light?'

'About five. We've an hour. Take this.' He gave her one of the pine branches. 'Light it in the fire if . . . when they come back.'

Amazon nodded, but said nothing. She didn't have to. They both knew they were going to be fighting for their lives.

29

Pack Attack

They came twenty minutes later, just as Amazon and Frazer were beginning to think that they were safe, and that the wolves had decided on other prey. It was hard to say what alerted them to the fact that the wolves were back – there was no obvious sound or sight or even smell, but they both knew that they were there, in the trees, beyond the light of the fire.

Without a word, Amazon and Frazer lit their pine branches in the fire. It seemed to Amazon that hers took an age to catch, but eventually the oily sap bubbled away, and the wood was alight.

The wolves circled closer, and the Trackers saw the gleam of their eyes in the flickering light, and heard their hot, urgent breath.

Frazer even convinced himself that he saw the original wolf – the sneaky scout slinking among them. He knew it was silly, but he took a personal dislike to that particular animal.

Amazon edged closer to Frazer. She had more

guts than any other teenager Frazer had ever met, but the truth was that he had simply been in this situation more often than she had. She hadn't come face to face with as many killers as he had.

Well, except for tigers, leopards, giant bears, killer squid and sharks . . .

'Got your back,' said Amazon, and Frazer knew why she had edged closer. He smiled.

'Good thinking. We've got to stay tight. They'll probably try to separate us, take us down one at a time.'

And then it began.

One wolf – a big pale creature, already in its thick winter coat – darted forward, baring its teeth in a savage snarl.

Frazer fought the panic that welled up in him like boiling water from a geyser. He wanted to turn and run, but he made himself lunge forward with the burning branch, again crying out a furious '*Yaaaaaahhhhh!*'

The big wolf squatted back on its haunches, growled and then fled. Its place was taken by two more. Frazer was relieved to find that Amazon had joined him again, matching his movements.

They waved their burning torches at the two newcomers, but did not dash forward. They both knew that they had to stay close to the shelter, with the young boy and younger bear. The two wolves kept their distance, lacking the courage to rush the flames, but nor did they flee.

'Look left,' said Amazon, but she didn't need to. Frazer had already sensed that a third wolf was there, trying to work its way in between them and the shelter.

'And there,' he replied, gesturing with the burning torch away to the right, where another – it was the slinker they had first encountered – was also prowling.

Together they edged back closer to the shelter. And then the grey wolf to the left made a dash, trying to get at the two little ones cowering under the pine boughs. It moved with slippery speed, and almost made it to the shelter and the easy pickings waiting there. But Amazon was on her toes and she just managed to thrust her burning branch into the wolf's flank. It yickered in pain, and then skittered away into the undergrowth, leaving behind it the stench of burnt hair.

The clash snuffed out Amazon's torch, but the other wolves seemed startled and spooked by what had happened to their brother, and backed away, letting Amazon and Frazer reach the shelter. Amazon looked quickly inside. There she saw Ben and Goldilocks clinging to each other, their eyes wide with terror.

Frazer relit Amazon's torch from his own. Each branch had burned down more than halfway. And they both knew that the flames were all that were keeping them alive.

'How long till dawn?' asked Amazon.

Frazer mumbled something back. It might have been, 'Too long.'

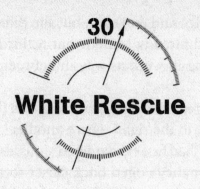

30

White Rescue

Rage.

Hunger.

Rage.

The feelings burned like sulphur in the beast's huge heart.

He had thundered through the forest, driven on by the sounds of the pack.

And so he had come.

There were seven in the pack. Four had attacked the place where the little white one lay. The others were spread around in the trees guarding the site. The other animals were there also, the ones who seemed to be helpers. Or at least who seemed not to be harmers. But if they tried to stop him . . . well, they could not stop him. He would take the little one.

But first, the wolves.

The first one knew nothing. It was watching the fight in the clearing by the water. Perhaps it heard at the last second, or smelled the strong, strange odour. But it had time only to twitch an ear, and then one swipe of a massive paw sent it sailing into the waiting branches of a tree, where it hung, limp and broken.

The white giant thundered on. The other guard wolves were aware of him now, and rushed to intercept. Two were before him. But now that they saw what he was, they quailed. The third joined them, which gave them courage. Their pack had dealt with bears almost as big as this in the past, driving them off kills, even if they had not had this strange ghostly appearance like a cloud with teeth and claws.

They darted in, and one managed a quick, sharp bite at the pale giant's leg. The bear swatted, but missed. Another bite, and another. It seemed that the wolves were just too fast, too well coordinated.

But then the bear heard a sound that was half whine, half growl coming from the clearing ahead. It was the little one. It needed him. Perhaps the helpers were not true helpers. Perhaps they were one with the wolves. He bounded forward, ignoring the bites of the attackers.

But one was too bold, and made a lunge at his throat. It paid dearly. The bear met bite with bite, and closed his great jaws round the smaller gape of the wolf. He bit, crunched and flicked the limp body away.

And now he was almost at the clearing. He could

see the eerie orange glow from the dying fire. All was chaos. The four wolves that were there now spun away from the humans and the baby bear, and ran into the trees to meet the challenge from their rear.

Among them was their leader, the alpha male of the pack. He was not the biggest or the strongest – that had been the pale grey beast, singed by Amazon. The leader was the small dark slinker.

It was not brute might that had made him the leader. It was his cunning. And he instantly understood the situation. Another wolf would have been astonished by the new arrival, so huge, so white in the pre-dawn. But this wolf saw that the bear was both a threat and an opportunity. It wanted to steal their meal, and that could not be allowed. But also the black wolf saw that it carried some secret hurt, a hurt perhaps of the soul more than the body, and so it was vulnerable. And a bear that big would feed the pack for many days.

And, once they had killed the newcomer, they could return for the smaller prey . . .

He barked and snarled his orders, injecting his courage and cunning into his pack mates.

They surrounded the bear. Five against one. They nipped and snapped. Each bite on its own seemed insignificant, and yet together they took their toll. The white giant's swats now lacked speed, and the harrying wolves were able to sway out of reach. Each time the bear tried to lunge towards its goal, the wolves attacked its flanks, drawing blood now and further weakening the big beast.

The fight rolled and surged through the forest. At the lip of a hill the bear finally fastened its jaws round one wolf, but lost its footing, and the whole snarling mass of fur and teeth rolled together down the slope.

All the time they were moving further away from the camp.

31

Flight Through the Forest

Amazon and Frazer could not see any of this clearly, but they certainly heard it.

'What the . . .!' exclaimed Frazer, peering into the trees at the first explosion of yelps, snarls and bellows.

They watched amazed as the wolves encircling them turned and ran towards the sound of battle.

'Is it the wolves fighting among themselves?' asked Amazon.

'No, I don't think so. It sounds like a bear, I guess. Or maybe a wolverine – we all know how feisty they can be . . .' Then Frazer's tone became urgent. 'But it might just have given us a chance. It's getting lighter now. If we hit the trail around the lake, we may be able to get clear by dawn. The wolves won't chase us in the day – it's just not their style.'

'But how can we cycle with Ben and the bear?'

'You take Goldilocks in her pack, and I'll give Ben

a ride on the back of my bike. But we need to do this *now*!'

As the ferocious noise of the battle ebbed and flowed, the Trackers hurled their gear into one pack, and bundled Goldilocks into the other.

'What's happening?' said a startled Ben, rubbing his eyes.

'We're going on a fun bike ride,' said Frazer.

'But I haven't got my bike!'

'You get to sit on the back of mine while I do all the work,' Frazer laughed. 'You've done this before, haven't you?'

'What, a backy? Yeah, lots of times. My brother Josh does it for me. He's nice.'

'OK, up you climb. And look, you get to carry my spear. Hold on tight!'

He turned to Amazon, who was ready to go, the bear on her back.

'You better take the lead, Zonnie. I'll keep up as best I can. And guess what?'

'What?'

'If you're up front, you get to use the helmet.'

He threw his helmet to Amazon. She caught it easily, thought about throwing it back, then put it on.

'I can hardly see the trail,' she said, peering at the ground.

'Just feel it, cuz, just feel it.'

Amazon rolled her eyes and hit the pedals. And prayed.

There was, in fact, just enough light to see by. They cycled round the beaver pond, and then into the trees. It was darker again when they were in the forest, and if there had been any roots or other obstacles across the trail then Amazon would have been in serious trouble, despite the helmet. But they lived a charmed life.

On one of the faster sections she heard Ben say '*Wheeeeeeeeee!*' and she wanted to crane round to see what they were up to. But this was not the sort of ride where you could take your eyes off the road.

Beyond the beaver pond the trail found the line of the stream again, generally working downwards, which made the cycling a lot easier. One of the good things about the ride was that Amazon had to concentrate everything on the task at hand, so her mind couldn't stray to what might be following them.

Behind her Frazer was a competent enough mountain biker to permit a little mind-wandering – even with a six-year-old kid sitting on his saddle. That part wasn't actually too tricky for Frazer. When you go down a mountain on a bike, you don't do much sitting anyway, so Frazer's leg muscles were easily up to the job.

But he didn't think he'd be able to outrun a pack

of wolves if they finished whatever it was that they'd been doing back at the lake and came after them. And so he was all ears for the sounds of pursuit.

There was something else on his mind as well. Through the trees he'd thought that he'd glimpsed what it was that the wolves were attacking. It was huge and it was white. No, not white – that was an illusion caused by its relative paleness against the black of the forest. It was a pale gold, like honey. For a split second he had thought it might have been Goldilocks's mother, but that was impossible. She was dead.

And then he thought that it might have been the spirit bear that had attacked Ben's hiking group. And that perhaps it had returned to finish the job.

And he knew something else: that bears could be incredibly persistent and single-minded. The wolf pack would not hunt them through the day, and by the next night the wolves would have found something else to occupy their quick minds. But the bear . . . if its mind was set on human flesh . . .

His thoughts were interrupted by Amazon shouting up ahead.

'At last,' she said, 'I can actually see what's in front of me. Hello morning!'

And now Frazer saw that she was right. The sun had not yet risen above the horizon, but the sky was light, and they were, for the time being, safe.

32

Ben's Story

Frazer cycled next to Amazon – there was just enough room for both bikes on the trail.

The trees were solid above them, but they could still sense that the skies were growing greyer. And then they heard a deep rumbling sound.

'Thunder . . .?' said Amazon, although it didn't sound quite like that.

'I don't think so,' said Frazer, listening intently. 'I think it might be a –'

'Hellycopter!' yelled Ben excitedly.

They all strained to try to see through the canopy. They even tried yelling. But they knew it was futile.

'They'll never see us,' said Frazer.

'Who do you think it is?' said Amazon.

'One of the search teams. Quick, let's try to get out of the trees so we can signal to them.'

They raced on down the trail, desperately searching for a break in the canopy. But soon the sound was gone and the trees were as thick as ever.

'You sure it really was a helicopter?' panted Amazon.

'I don't know,' groaned Frazer. 'Could have been thunder after all. Maybe it was just wishful thinking. Your mind can play tricks when you're in the wilderness. Anyway, I think we all need a rest.'

They had been pedalling for an hour and even Frazer's steely thighs were aching.

'I wanna go pee-pee,' added Ben. 'And I'm hungry.'

'OK, little guy,' said Frazer, 'time for a comfort break.'

They pulled over and sat on the ground, exhausted. Amazon took Goldilocks out of the pack and fed her a handful of trail mix as she looked anxiously back down the path.

'Have we put enough distance between us and the wolves?'

'If it was still night, I'd say no. But the dawn means we're pretty safe, I reckon. They'll be going back to the den. Some of them at least . . .'

'Some . . .? Oh, you mean because of the fight. You still think it was a bear?'

Frazer nodded. He didn't think that there was any sense in scaring her about the big white beast he had seen. Besides, with a bit of luck, they would make it back to the Tracker camp later that day.

But still he thought that it was perhaps the time to ask Ben about his ordeal.

He made some space next to him on the ground and beckoned the boy over.

'Hey, Ben. I was kinda wondering if you remembered anything about the night you got split up from your mom and dad. Cos you know you're a big star, don't you?'

'Huh?'

'Yep, a big star. You've been on the TV and the radio and all over the internet.'

'Really?'

'Really.'

'My friend Suzie Jo is gonna be so jealous. She wants to be on the TV more than anything.'

'So you want to tell me what you remember?'

'Well, we were walking all day and I was tired. My mommy and daddy had an argument about me. My mommy said they never shoulda brought me because I was too young, and my daddy said it was good, and that I'd grow up fast. And then we camped. We had sausages to eat. I told my daddy I wanted to share a tent with my friend Pete and his mommy, and they said I could, probably so they could argue some more. And I went to sleep real fast because I was all walked-out, and then I woke up and everyone was screaming.

'Pete's mommy went outside and then Pete went out too. I was looking for my other shoe when the tent all exploded and then the monster was there, like a giant Goldilocks, but more fiercer and not as cute. And then someone fired a gun and there was more yelling and I don't know how, but I was running and running and running and I ran forever because

I didn't want to get eat by the bear. And then I climbed up high in a tree, because I'm the best at climbing in my school, and I waited for my mommy and daddy to come, but they didn't. Then I fell asleep in the tree.

'When I woke up, it was daytime and I stayed up in the tree yelling as loud as I could, but they didn't come. And I waited nearly all day because I was frightened to go down in case the bear was there, but my mommy still didn't come so I climbed down and then I walked a long time until I saw a light and I thought it was my mommy and daddy, but it wasn't – it was just you.'

There was a little pause after that, finally filled by Frazer saying, 'I think you are definitely the bravest boy in Canada, and I think you will be so famous when we get home that everyone in the whole of North America will have heard about you and there'll be photographers outside your school, and you'll get invited on to talk shows, and they might even make a movie about you.'

'I hope so. That'll teach Suzie Jo a lesson for being so snooty. And I'm hungry. Can I have some food now?'

'Well, I guess it is breakfast time,' smiled Frazer.

And so together they ate the very last of the trail food. It wasn't enough to satisfy any of them, so Frazer and Amazon gave most to the bear and the boy.

'Right,' said Frazer, 'from now on we live off the land. Luckily we're here when there's plenty to forage. Berries. Mushrooms, er . . . Did I already mention the berries?'

'I can eat berries for a day or two,' replied Amazon, 'but I'm not so sure about these two little guys.'

'My mommy always gives me ice cream with blueberries,' said Ben wistfully.

Amazon again remembered how hungry the little boy must be.

'I promise you you'll be eating berries and ice cream by this time tomorrow,' she said and gave him a hug.

'My bear wants some too or she'll be jealous,' said the boy.

'OK. Two scoops each, no more.'

'Three!'

'You drive a hard bargain. But three it is.' Amazon turned to Frazer. 'I'm right, aren't I? I mean, we'll get back today?'

'We should do,' he replied, without the easy optimism Amazon was both hoping for and half expecting. 'If we can find the route. The trouble is that we've come a long way in the wrong direction, and it can be easy to get yourself lost in the woods. We need to get to higher ground so I can see where we are and plot the way back. You ready to head out?'

Amazon nodded. She put the protesting little bear

in the backpack and hoisted it on to her shoulders. Frazer remembered how surprisingly heavy the cub was.

'You sure you're OK?' he asked.

She smiled. 'I'll still be going when you're begging for mercy.'

They both laughed then, the slow-gathering but ultimately near hysterical laughter of those who have endured terrible events.

'What's funny?' asked Ben a couple of times, his blue eyes wide with astonishment.

'You are, monkey-face,' said Frazer and ruffled his hair.

And then he looked at Amazon again, and saw that the laughter and the jokes had hidden a deeper sadness.

'You're thinking about your mom and dad, aren't you?' he said.

'Always.'

'We'll keep looking for signs on the way back. And then,' he added, his affectionate gaze taking in Ben and Goldilocks, 'when we've got the kids settled, we'll be back out here, and we'll find them. We really will.'

Amazon nodded, but had to turn away to hide the glistening of her eyes.

'Come on, then,' said Frazer. 'That way looks like up to me.'

And once again they set off to look for higher ground.

33

Higher Ground

And then things got both easier and much tougher. It was fully light by now, which not only made it possible to see where they were going, but also banished the terrors of the night. Amazon found it hard to believe that they had been attacked by a pack of wolves. Weren't wolves the stuff of nightmares and not reality?

But the relative ease ended when Frazer, through a break in the solid canopy of pines, saw a hill looming up away to one side of the trail.

'Right, guys, we've got a choice. I'm going to climb up there to find out exactly where we are, and which way we have to head back to civilization. I'm hoping that either I'll be able to see the way back to our old camp or, with a bit of luck, I might just catch a glimpse of a road or a ranger station or something like that. Hey, I might even see that helicopter again. But we don't all need to go up. If you want, you can stay here and wait for me. That'll certainly be quicker than us all climbing up there.'

He pointed up the steep slopes of the hill. It was a little lower than Mount Humboldt, but then there had just been the two of them and their bikes; now they had passengers.

Amazon looked at Ben and Goldilocks. They were looking right back at her, hope and trust in the eyes of the boy, curiosity and hunger in the eyes of the bear.

'I think it's best if we all stick together,' she said. 'The truth is that you're better than me in these woods – and yes, it's pretty hard for me to admit that you're better at *anything* than I am. But, if something happens, I want it to happen when you're there.'

Frazer nodded, acknowledging the compliment. And the common sense.

'But don't get cocky,' Amazon continued. 'I can still kick your ass, as you Americans so vulgarly put it.'

'Amazon Hunt, you are a piece of work,' laughed Frazer. 'When this is all over, we'll put that to the test.'

'Bring it on.'

The lower part of the hill remained thickly wooded, and there was no way that they could cycle. They pushed their bikes through the trees, with Goldilocks still riding in Amazon's backpack, and Ben sitting on Frazer's saddle, his arms stretched forward to grip the handlebars.

The forest was still eerily quiet. They heard the drumming of a woodpecker and the screech of some bird of prey – a goshawk, thought Amazon – as it streaked through the branches above them, but they saw nothing.

After half an hour, they broke through the treeline and saw that they had climbed a fair way.

Frazer surveyed the rocky slope ahead.

'Hate to break this to you, Ben, but you're going to have to walk from now on. Have you climbed a mountain before?'

'Sure, lots of mountains. And I once climbed up on to the garage roof to get my ball back.'

They climbed on. The ground was solid rock from this point – not the loose shale and boulders that they had encountered on their ascent of Humboldt. Their eyes and ears strained for any sight or sound of the returning helicopter, but soon the toughness of the climb made it difficult to think of anything except each hard step.

The going became so tough that it was obvious to Frazer after another hundred metres that, whatever Amazon thought, they couldn't all make it. Ben was brave and determined, but his little legs weren't made for this sort of terrain. He kept falling over, and soon his knees were scraped raw. Frazer gave him a piggyback, but there was no way he could get to the top with that kind of burden.

Things were tough for Amazon as well. She was

carrying a now rather agitated bear on her back as well as pushing her bike up the slope.

'Guys,' Frazer announced, including Ben and Goldilocks in his gaze, 'I think it's time I went on alone. You can stay here and look after the bikes. I can get up to the top and have a look around in half an hour. If we all struggle on, it's gonna take at least two.'

Amazon saw the sense in this. She also saw a flaw.

'I think you should be the one to stay with Ben and Goldilocks,' she said. 'If anything turns up, you'll be much more able to defend them with that spear of yours.'

'Hey, it's my spear now!' protested Ben. 'You gave it to me fair and square. If you take it back, I'm gonna tell everyone that you're a big cheater.'

'Chill out, Ben, the spear's all yours. Any bad old bear comes along and I'll teach it some karate.'

Frazer performed a couple of fancy kicks and chops, which made Ben giggle.

It also showed to Amazon that she had won the argument. She shrugged off the bear-pack with enormous relief, and handed it over to Frazer. 'OK,' she said, 'I'm tired of being mummy bear – your turn to play daddy.'

Frazer was looking thoughtful. 'Something just occurred to me, Zonnie. Dad went the wrong way to look for Ben and the big bad bear, but the other hunters – the ones out in the woods looking to kill any spirit bear that comes along – well, they might not be that far away. You should keep an eye out for them too. If we tell them that we've got Ben safe then they'll call off the hunt. Not to mention help us get out of here.'

'But are they the kind of people who would give up on the chance to shoot things just because there's no need?' replied Amazon.

Frazer shrugged. 'Fair point. But keep your eyes peeled anyway. And look after these –' He handed Amazon his beautiful binoculars.

Amazon nodded, hung the binoculars round her neck and began climbing.

'You be careful,' called out Frazer after her.

She turned back to wave, and saw him below, struggling like a dad in the mall to keep control of two unruly kids. She turned back to the hilltop and walked on, smiling.

34

The Top

It wasn't half an hour. It took Amazon a gruelling hour to reach the top. It was one of those very annoying big hills (or small mountains) that is made up of a series of ridges, each one looking convincingly like it might be the last. She never really had to do any proper climbing, but she often had to scramble on hands and knees to get up the trickier sections.

What made it all rather worse was that, for the first time since they'd flown into the mountains, it began to rain. And with the rain the temperature fell. Climbing on dry rocks can be fun: climbing on wet rocks never, ever is. Amazon began to regret that she hadn't brought proper climbing boots, or at least some stout walking shoes, rather than just her trainers. And she was cold.

She looked at her hands. They were filthy. She had planned to wash in the beaver pond that morning, but being attacked by wolves can drive little issues like personal hygiene out of your mind.

She kept checking behind her, but the same system of ridges that obscured the summit also soon took Frazer and the others beyond her sight. She hoped they'd all be OK in the rain. She'd grown very fond of the little boy and the little bear in the short time they'd been together.

The next ridge was the toughest so far. It was steep and wet, and the cold had grown more intense. Winter was coming, she sensed. Up here there was a constant nagging wind that cut through her clothing. Her TRACKS expedition outfit was waterproof and windproof, but Amazon really wished she had a couple more layers to keep her warm.

The last few metres to the top of the ridge were horrendous. It now suddenly did feel a little like real mountain climbing, as she hauled herself up, needing to find both hand- and footholds. She looked quickly back again, and was delighted to see, for the first time in ages, the distant figures of Frazer, Ben and Goldilocks. They were playing a game of tag down there. She thought about shouting and waving, but she needed both her hands to avoid a nasty fall.

She finally scrambled to the top of the ridge, and looked to see how difficult the next one would be.

And what she saw made her sigh.

There was nothing. Or, rather, there was everything. She was at the top. The wide world fell away in every direction. From up here Amazon could see the endless forests of pine and fir. She could see dozens of lakes, and countless streams and rivers. She could see the flatter land beyond the range of the coastal mountains. And there, behind her, perhaps some nine or ten miles away, was the grey magnificence of Mount Humboldt. She carefully took her bearings. It was due west.

Perfect.

No complications, nothing to forget or muddle up. Amazon saw that, if they followed one of the streams that flowed not far from where Frazer and the others had stopped, they would be taken almost straight back to that mountain. And once there it would be easy to pick up the trail back to camp and the reassuring presence of Uncle Hal. It was a long road back, and a tough one, but knowing that they were going the right way was in itself a huge boost: nothing saps the energy like the fear that you've taken a wrong turning and all your efforts are futile.

She'd almost forgotten the binoculars hanging round her neck. She hadn't needed them to work out the way back, but now she used them to scour the land for any sign of life – whether it be the hunters skulking out there to kill, or, as she dreamed, her parents. She could imagine them sitting together round a fire, arm in arm, thinking of her just as she was dreaming of them.

But it was impossible. The world was so huge. There were so many thousands of square miles of wilderness. The binoculars were actually worse than just looking with her own two eyes – they took her in too close. It would take years to check out the full view like this. She let them fall back around her neck. She had a last look at the view, taking in all its magnificence and grandeur under the glowering grey skies.

OK, enough grandeur, Amazon told herself. It was going to be a long journey back to the camp, and she had no intention of spending another night with the wolves for company. She began the awkward journey back down the hillside.

And then she stopped.

Something had registered with her subconscious mind. What was it? She had already clambered down a couple of tricky metres. She glanced back at the summit, thought about ignoring the little mind-worm in her head and carrying on back to the others, groaned and climbed again those nasty, knuckle-grazing metres.

She stood again on the flat top of the mountain – a space no bigger than a kitchen table – and turned slowly round, trying to bring into focus what it was that was needling her.

There.

In a valley between two lower hills. Something strange about the trees. Something not natural.

She put the binoculars to her eyes again and twisted the focusing ring. Blurred and then sharp.

Suddenly the trees that had been so far away seemed almost close enough to touch.

Yes, there definitely seemed to be a pattern. The trees had been cut and arranged in a way that looked man-made. It almost reminded Amazon of Frazer's lean-to shelter that had protected them the previous night. The branches of the spruce and pine seemed to form a roof. A roof over what? She refocused the binoculars. There, a glint of something just projecting from the boughs. She took the binoculars away and looked with her naked eyes. Was there also a lighter grey showing up against the slate grey of the sky? Something that could be a wisp of smoke?

Once more she looked through the binoculars.

And now she was sure that she knew what it was, lying there beneath the deliberate camouflage of the branches.

A tangle of wreckage. A tangle of wreckage in which Amazon could make out something long and slender . . .

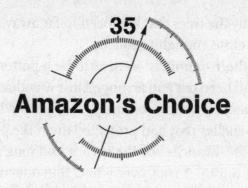

35

Amazon's Choice

It was a plane.

A plane that had crashed.

And there, above it, a tendril of smoke from a dying fire.

That could mean only one thing . . .

Her head spun and she so nearly fell from that flat mountaintop. She boiled and bubbled with excitement, hope and fear.

She looked towards Frazer and the others. They seemed so far away. But something – some special sense – told her that Frazer was looking at her. She waved her arms frantically. And yes, he waved back. He could see her. She screamed at the top of her voice.

'PLANE! MY PARENTS' PLANE!'

Frazer waved again. She heard his voice calling back, but couldn't make out what he was saying.

Amazon looked back to the plane. The slope on that side of the mountain was smooth and easy. She could literally run down that hill, the way she had countless times as a girl in the English countryside, right into the waiting arms of her dad. She could get down there to her parents in minutes. The alternative was the difficult and dangerous and time-consuming journey back down the tough side to the others, and then the agonizingly slow trek round the mountain to the crash site. And what if something happened to Ling-Mei and Roger in that time? There were bears, wolves, cougars . . . She would never forgive herself.

She waved again at Frazer, getting his attention. She pointed back down to where the wreck was. She tried to signal that she was going to go straight down to it, and that he should follow the line of the mountain round to meet her. Again Frazer waved back.

It was enough for Amazon. He'd understood. He would meet her there. It's what she wanted to believe. Without another thought, she plunged down towards the plane, towards her longed-for reunion with her mum and dad.

36
Frazer Left Holding the Baby

Frazer looked up at Amazon. The steady drizzle was in his eyes. He wiped them clear with the sleeve of his jacket. His cousin was waving, and he sensed that she was shouting something. Was it a warning? He waved and shouted back.

'Are you OK, Zonnie? What can you see?'

He could tell that she was excited. Or agitated. Or frightened.

'Can we go home now, please,' whined Ben. He was soaked to the skin and shivering. Frazer had tried to keep them all warm by playing tag, but the little boy was even more tired than he was cold.

'Soon, little guy,' he said. 'Real soon. Amazon is just trying to find the right path. You just carry on being a brave soldier. Remember, you're the guy with the spear.'

Ben looked at the spear in his hand, and then threw it away.

'Don't want the spear. Don't want you. Don't want Zomazon. Want my mommy and my daddy.'

The little boy then cast himself down on the bleak, shelterless hillside and cried his heart out, his sobs echoing off the hard rock.

Frazer moved to comfort him. He got there in a second, but Goldilocks was there before him, nuzzling at Ben's neck and face. Frazer crouched over both of them, trying to share his warmth, using his body to protect them from the rain.

When he next looked up to where Amazon had been at the top of the mountain, he saw nothing but huge grey skies, and the looming black of storm clouds. Even as he looked, he felt a change in the texture of the rain that had been falling. It was harder now – not in the sense that more of it was falling. No, it was harder because it had undergone the subtle change from rain to sleet.

And those black clouds above them could mean only one thing. That the sleet was going to turn to snow. The first big fall of the season.

'Where are you, Zonnie?' he said to himself, hoping that he would see her again soon as she came over one of the ridges.

'Where are you?'

37

The Wreck

Amazon didn't climb, walk or even run down the side of the mountain.

She flew.

Her feet moved so quickly that they barely made contact with the ground. It was a miracle that she didn't trip or slip and fall. Had she done so, it might well have been fatal. She could have slid, gathering momentum until she crashed into one of the boulders that littered the slope, and broken her neck.

But this was not Amazon Hunt's time to die.

She was down the mountain in twenty minutes. Another ten took her to the opening of the gully where the wreck was. The smoke from the fire was gone now, either obscured by the trees or drowned out by the rain.

No, not rain, sleet now.

She called out, her voice harsh and cracked with emotion.

'Mum, Dad, I'm here! I'm here!'

She felt like a tiny child again, in need of their comfort and protection, but also like a hero, their rescuer, the person who had come to save them.

'Mummy!' she screamed again, as she ran through a stream, the freezing water splashing unnoticed over her legs. She couldn't see the wreck any longer, but she knew that it was here, just beyond this bend in the gully.

Her lungs ached, but ached in some remote place, some unimportant part of her, so she ignored the discomfort and sped on.

And there it was, hidden beneath the overhanging branches: the tangle of torn metal.

The plane was tiny – smaller than the little floatplane that Uncle Hal had flown them in on. Amazon ran past the wheels of the undercarriage, which had been torn off in the crash-landing. A crash-landing she was now imagining all too vividly. She saw that the windscreen had been shattered, and the tail section completely sheared off.

'Mum! Dad!' she called again. But already she knew that her shouts were futile.

There was nobody here. She was alone, beside a wrecked plane in the middle of the Canadian wilderness. The sleet struck heavily against her face and mingled with the tears. It was hopeless. So hopeless. Her parents were dead and gone.

Dead and gone.

38

They Follow

It had taken Frazer half an hour to realize that Amazon wasn't coming down the mountain. Or at least wasn't coming down on *this* side of the mountain. He replayed again the gestures she had made, tried to extract some sense from the words she had screamed down at him – words carried away by the wind.

She seemed to be pointing down to the far side of the mountain. Had she seen something? Had she been trying to tell him to meet her there? Or was she warning him against some approaching danger?

Whatever it was, he couldn't wait here. The sleet was now steady and turning to snow. The bear and the boy were freezing. If they stayed on this bleak mountainside, they were going to die.

But it wasn't just that. Frazer wasn't a waiting around kind of person. He had to find shelter. Build a fire. And find Amazon.

He looked at Ben and Goldilocks, huddled together, both looking as wretched as each other.

'Well, guys, I think it's time we did something rather special. How many times do you think a kid and a bear and a teenager have ridden together on a mountain bike?'

'I d-don't know,' said Ben. For the first time in ages he sounded interested. 'Maybe n-not ever?'

'You're right. Maybe never. But we're going to do it now.'

Five minutes later, Frazer was wearing the backpack slung round his front, so that the little bear's inquisitive face was right in his. Ben was sitting on the saddle again, his arms round Frazer.

'OK, guys, you hang on tight. We're off-trail now, so this is going to be a bumpy ride. You up for it?'

'You bet!' said Ben, who did sound like he was enjoying himself.

Goldilocks licked Frazer's face.

'Eew! Tell you one thing, little lady, we are so going to brush your teeth when we get home.'

And, with that, Frazer kicked off. He intended to travel round the base of the mountain to meet Amazon on the other side. It was the only thing he could think to do. He would stay just above the treeline, trying to keep to relatively flat ground.

If he didn't bump into Amazon where he was hoping to find her then he'd build up a great big fire and that would let her know where he was.

It might not have been the greatest plan in the history of the world, but at least it was one. And any plan was better than no plan, unless, as his old friend Bluey used to say, that plan is covering your naked body in honey and rolling around on a nest of fire ants while singing 'Yankee Doodle Dandy'.

39

The Bear Again

His wounds were deep, but not mortal. The fight had raged through the forest. Up hills and down hills; splashing through icy lakes; crashing through briars and brambles.

He had taken many bites, but he had also inflicted much hurt upon the others. Finally the dark one had come, waiting until he thought the pale giant was almost spent. He was lying down, the blood oozing into the wet earth from a hundred wounds. The black wolf had hissed words in the wolf tongue, words of threat and also of relish. They were going to start feeding upon him while he still breathed.

But, when the black wolf leapt at his throat, the bear found the strength for one last mighty swat, and the huge paw with its great curving claws dealt the wolf a blow that would have been mortal had the wily animal not swerved at the last second, and so took the hit on the shoulder and not his head.

The other wolves, seeing their leader vanquished,

hurried away, leaving the great bear to pant and bleed and, slowly, recover.

In an hour he was able to begin the search for the camp. He followed first his own trail, and then the smell of the fire came back to him. Now he galloped through the forest, forgetting stealth.

He burst into the clearing . . .

And there was nothing. Nothing except for the dead bones of the fire, and the shelter made from pine branches. The bear raged and rampaged, smashing the shelter, scattering the ashes of the fire. A huge pressure built up within his breast. He would find them. There would be revenge.

His nose got to work, and soon he located the strange scent trail. It was a mix of things. Some living, some dead. There was still the smell of the small bear, but it was so faint. That didn't matter. The smell of the human killers was strong enough to follow. He bounded after them, death in his heart.

40

Amazon Explores

It took fifteen minutes for Amazon to cry herself out. Her mind was blasted with images of her beloved mother and father. Of them all playing together in the park. Of the heartbreak of the many partings, as they set off on another expedition; of the corresponding joy when they returned.

Her grief didn't have any more of a basis than the fact that she had been convinced that she would see her father's shy smile and her mother's beautiful face again, and had found, in reality, an empty plane and a deserted campsite.

And, of course, there was no indication that it had even been her parents' aircraft. There were probably dozens of crashed planes scattered across this forest. This one might have been here for years. The fire might have been lit by campers making use of the site.

No, there was no hope, no hope at all that Amazon would see her parents again.

But then, as the torrent of grief subsided, she began to think. And to explore. And to hope. This was exactly where Hal had thought her parents would be. It was possible that they had simply left for a day of foraging, that they would come back.

She looked into the cabin of the aircraft. There were signs that people had been living there. Two sleeping bags were arranged on the floor. And something else. She had a very strong feeling of a certain sequence of events. There had been the crash, which had damaged the plane and smashed up the interior. But there was no blood, no obvious signs of fatal injuries. That was good.

Then there had been a clean-up. Some sort of domestic harmony had been restored here. There were even dried flowers in a cup on the broken dashboard of the plane.

It meant that whoever had crashed had survived. And then had stayed here for a while.

But then there was a final archaeological layer of chaos. The attempt to make the plane a comfortable habitation had been disrupted. There was mess everywhere. The sleeping bags had, by the look of them, been cut open and the filling of downy feathers scattered around.

Amazon climbed out of the plane, more mystified than ever. She went back to the dying fire. There was still a little warmth from it, although the sleet had killed the last of the embers. A little wall of rocks and turf had been built up round the fire, as if to hide its flames from the world, which seemed strange.

Then she explored further from the plane.

Wherever she went she saw signs of what had been a tidy campsite suddenly turned upside down. Logs from a once neatly stacked woodpile were scattered and kicked around. And, nearby, she found an empty rucksack, with the contents strewn over the ground.

Amazon tried to remember if she had seen her parents with a rucksack like it. She couldn't, but it was quite new, and so they might have bought it since she had last been with them. The stuff that had been tipped out had blown far and wide. She went around to each piece – a glove here, a T-shirt there – and tried to recognize them, even smelling them to see if they retained any essence of her parents.

There was one blue shirt that she was sure her mother had bought for her father, two Christmases ago. But it was so hard to tell.

Amazon went back to the fire. On the way she came across an area of tussocky grass that was weirdly flattened. It was a circle perhaps ten metres across. She wondered what could have caused this. A herd of animals of some kind? Uncle Hal had said that there were forest bison up here – could they do this?

But it was too cold for such speculation. And it wasn't going to help Amazon find her parents. She was shivering now. And she suddenly remembered

Frazer and the bear and the boy. She had rushed away from the mountaintop without thinking of them.

Had Frazer understood her signalled message?

Well, he wasn't here, so probably not. He was almost certainly still waiting for her, a long trek round the base of the mountain. In the continuing sleet that was now turning to snow, proper snow with big flakes floating and swirling in complicated patterns.

There was no point moping. Her parents weren't here. She would go and meet the others, and they would somehow try to make it back to the first camp before nightfall.

Amazon put her cold hands next to the fire to try to extract the last of the warmth from the damp ashes before she set off.

And then she heard the roar.

41

Golden Terror

Roar wasn't quite the right word for the sound that Amazon Hunt heard coming from the monster that towered over her. Roar suggests only power, might, anger. But this bellow had more pain in it than any of those.

Amazon, still crouching by the dead fire, was looking up at the biggest living creature she had ever been close to, with the exception of the elephants at London Zoo.

And something rather strange happened.

One part of her brain surged with blinding, deafening, paralysing terror. That was the sane part of her mind, the part that knew that she was about to be torn apart and probably eaten by a creature big enough to break the windows on the top deck of a bus. But another part of her brain, the insane, bizarro, loop-the-loop part, remained astonishingly cool and lucid. That part of her brain managed to observe this mega-beast with painful clarity.

She knew, of course, that it was a bear, but after that she was perplexed. Like the beautiful spirit bears, this was a pale golden colour. But Amazon could see immediately that this was no spirit bear – which was, after all, only a subspecies of black bear. The biggest black bears were not even half the size of this monster.

Although more yellow than white, its colour made her think of a polar bear. And it did look a little like one. But two things ruled that out. The shape was wrong. Its neck was broad and thick, not long and sinuous, like a polar bear. And the face was too wide, and the muzzle too short. Most of all, this bear had a huge hump of muscle on its back, between the shoulder blades. She knew that that meant it must be a grizzly. But, even apart from the colour, there was something distinctly *ungrizzlyish* about this bear.

And no grizzly, she thought, had ever been quite this big.

The bear had been standing on its back legs, staring at her. She'd read that they did that not to intimidate, but simply so they could get a better look at what they were about to attack. And now, with a sound that she felt in the balls of her feet, the huge bear crunched back down on to all fours.

It snorted twice, pulling her scent deep into its sensitive nose, and then it began to walk towards her. Not a charge, and not an amble – this was a purposeful, businesslike walk. It was the walk of a bear that has work to do. It was the walk of a bear about to eat.

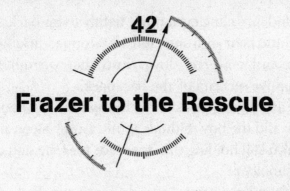

42

Frazer to the Rescue

Frazer's journey had been . . . *tricky*, to say the least. The main problem was the baby bear in his face. Goldilocks was clearly famished, and seemed to think that licking his mouth might make him regurgitate some goodies.

It turned out to be surprisingly hard to steer a mountain bike over rough terrain through a sleet shower when a bear is licking your face.

But the last thing Frazer wanted to do was stop – getting moving in the first place was the hardest thing of all, and he wasn't going to sacrifice his momentum just to avoid a mouthful of baby bear drool.

He looked quickly up to the peak of the mountain a couple of times to try to work out if he had reached the spot yet that he guessed, or rather hoped, Amazon had indicated. He was thinking he must be close when he heard the bellow.

It froze his blood, far more quickly and effectively than the freezing rain had done. He felt the little boy behind him cling even more tightly to his back, and the little bear in front suddenly stopped licking his face and cowered down into the warmth and deceptive security of the backpack.

Frazer briefly considered his options. He had the bear and the boy to think about. And his cousin.

'You still holding that spear for me?' he said over his shoulder.

'It's my spear now,' came a small, pinched voice. 'But you can borrow it.'

Frazer cycled with new strength and speed towards the sound of the bear.

43

The Stand-off

Amazon grabbed a log from the fire, and stood to face the bear. The end of the log had turned to charcoal and, as she waved it before her, a tiny ember glowed briefly, leaving a wisp of smoke.

It wasn't enough to deter the bear. It carried on walking towards her.

Amazon reviewed everything she had ever read or heard about bear attacks. Never get anywhere near a mother and cubs. That she knew, first hand. And it was of no use to her now.

Try climbing a tree to escape a grizzly – black bears can climb, adult grizzlies struggle.

But don't bother trying to outrun a bear to the tree – it'll beat you every time, and running will only ever trigger its predator-prey response.

Use bear spray. Again, useless – she didn't have any.

Make yourself look big.

She tried that. But compared to the giant walking

towards her, even a full-grown man would look puny. Heck, so would most bears.

Talk soothingly to the bear, as you back slowly away. She'd seen Hal Hunt do that.

Amazon tried to speak, but nothing came out.

Anyway, that was when a bear felt threatened by you. This bear didn't feel threatened. This bear *was* the threat.

If you get attacked by a bear with cubs, play dead. Otherwise, fight back.

Well, that's what Amazon was doing now. There were accounts she'd read of bears being deterred by a thwack on the nose. That was her only hope. If she had the chance, she'd ram the smouldering log right up its snout.

She wasn't giving up without a fight.

44

The Cavalry

Frazer took the gentle rise just a little too quickly. It was a classic situation for a dirt-bike jump, and he'd have aced it in normal circumstances.

But these weren't normal circumstances. He had a boy on the back and a bear on the front.

And a monster before him.

He saw it while he was still in mid-air.

It was moving towards Amazon, who was standing resolutely, a blackened log in her hands.

His first thought was 'polar bear'.

His second, 'albino grizzly'.

His third, '*AAAAAAAHHHHHHHHHHH!*'

Then they landed. Or rather crashed.

Luckily they touched down in an area of boggy ground, its surface a mass of moss and wet leaves. If they'd hit rock then some serious damage would have been caused.

Frazer managed to half turn as he went over the handlebars so that he did not crush the little bear.

Ben fell sprawling face first into the mulch and wasn't badly hurt and – for the time being – was still too shocked to cry. The spear he'd been carrying flew from his hand.

Frazer was winded, but his mind remained clear. He ran over to the boy.

'Stay here,' he said, pressing the boy down into the ground. They had fallen just behind a rocky outcrop, high enough to conceal the boy from the bear if he kept low. 'Be absolutely quiet. And, whatever you do, don't look, or get up. Got that?'

'Uh-huh.'

'And take care of Goldilocks.'

Frazer quickly unhooked himself from the bear-laden backpack and thrust it down next to Ben.

Then, scooping up the spear as he went, he ran towards Amazon, screaming at the top of his voice.

The bear was now five metres away from Amazon. She had turned, her astonishment, Frazer could see, mingled with the seed of hope. In a couple of seconds he was at her side, and together the cousins confronted the advancing bear, she with her club, he with his home-made spear.

'Thought you'd never get here,' said Amazon, from the side of her mouth.

Frazer tried to think of a quick, witty comeback, but then decided that it was probably more important to stay alive.

'You go for the nose,' he said.

'Duh!' replied Amazon, as though she'd been fighting giant yellow bears all her life.

'And I'll go for the eye. If it takes me down, grab the kid and run and don't look back. Head for the mountain. Find the trail and don't stop till you're home.'

Amazon looked at him, smiled a brief but warm smile and then together they faced the bear.

45

The Monster Revealed

And now Frazer had the chance to really look at the huge animal that was approaching them he found his terror almost exactly matched by his awe. It was the biggest bear he had ever seen, but also clearly unlike any other bear in the world. It was a completely new species. Something in between a polar bear and a grizzly. It was a . . .

And then it dawned on him exactly what it was.

But that knowledge would not help them now. The bear had been startled, no – that was too strong a word – it had been mildly surprised when he had exploded off the bike and into its world. It had paused for a moment or two, raised its massive head – longer than a grizzly's, rounder than a polar bear's – to take a reassuring sniff. But then it had come on again. It was getting two for the price of one, like a grocery store special offer.

It was beginning to move up to attack speed when suddenly it stopped dead in its tracks.

It had been distracted by a noise.

Goldilocks was bleating. Still trapped in the rucksack, the little golden bear was struggling to get free, making loud complaints. Ben was trying hard to comfort the cub, but it wasn't working. The boy didn't know what to do to calm the creature.

And the giant bear was now ambling in their direction.

'Oh no . . .' said Frazer.

'Ha! Here!' he yelled, but the big bear ignored him. It was running now towards the rock behind which the boy and the baby bear were hiding.

Frazer ran to try to intercept it, and he sensed that Amazon was right there with him. He carried on screaming, waving his arms wildly.

But it was too late. Bears run faster than people. Much faster. That's all there was to it.

The great pale monster reached the little outcrop of rock. Still the sounds of the struggling cub came from beyond it.

'Run!' screamed Frazer, metres behind the bear. 'Ben, run, please, run for your life!'

It was the only hope – that the big bear would attack the little bear first, giving Ben the chance to get away. It was a desperate hope. And probably forlorn. The bear stepped easily over the rock. It bent and it seemed to Frazer that it was biting something. He jumped and reached the rock seconds after the bear.

And then he stopped.

From the trees away to the left something came hurtling.

Amazon saw it first.

It was moving with a weird jerky gallop, as if it were carrying some terrible injury, but an injury that love or hate had striven to overcome. It was similar in colour to the yellow giant. But the shape was different. Rounder. And so much smaller. But the bellow it was emitting was not small at all. It was the cry of a mother, out to save her baby.

But, as Frazer had already seen, it was too late.

46

The Three Bears

Amazon was a stride behind Frazer. She stopped next to him on the low rock and looked down. What she saw amazed her.

The huge yellow bear was gently nuzzling at Goldilocks. As she watched, he slipped his muzzle inside the bag and eased it open, so the baby could get free. The two sniffed at each other and then the baby put its paw up and touched the other bear's face. The big bear then delicately nuzzled at the baby.

But only for a second, because then, with a final grunting roar, the third bear arrived.

'*It . . . it's the mother,*' said Frazer, astonished. 'She must have somehow survived that rockfall. She was obviously knocked out when she was buried, but then came round and somehow managed to follow us here.'

'But she's hurt . . . badly hurt . . .' said Amazon.

But, as if to deny that, the mother bear crashed into the giant, which must have been at least four times her weight. Frazer was convinced that the huge bear would retaliate and the mother would stand no chance against him.

But the massive animal backed away from the mother. Backed away and then lay down, first on its side and then on its back. The female staggered over – clearly her mad charge had used up her remaining energy. She bit at the bigger bear, but not savagely. It was more like a reprimand. Like a mother telling off her son – almost.

Still the huge bear cringed beneath her. And then she saw her cub, and the two of them bleated out their delight, while the huge male looked on, almost bashfully.

Amazon and Frazer took the opportunity to move quietly to Ben. Amazon picked up the little boy and hugged him.

'What's going on?' she whispered to Frazer. 'And what kind of bear is that anyway?'

'I'm pretty sure it's a hybrid – half grizzly, half polar bear. I read something about there being one or two of them in zoos. And they've started to turn up in the wild. It's even got a name . . . a pizzly . . . no, a grolar, that's it. It's going to get more common because of global warming, which is bringing the two species closer together.'

'But that doesn't explain what's going on now . . . Why aren't they fighting? And why didn't he kill the cub? I thought that's what they did . . .?'

'I know, it's bizarre. I can only think that . . . well, maybe he's all alone. He's not like any other bears, but he's the same colour, almost, as the Kermode bears. Maybe he thinks he's one of them. And the other thing is that he might only be a kid.'

'*A kid?* But he's enormous!'

'Sometimes when you get a hybrid the genes that limit growth get turned off. That's why a liger – a half tiger half lion – is much bigger than either of its parents. So maybe that's what's going on here. He's just a big baby. He lost his mother, and now he thinks he's found one.'

Amazon looked again. And it did, in fact, appear exactly as Frazer said. The mother spirit bear had Goldilocks sheltered between her front paws, and the massive grolar was trying to butt in, pushing his nose towards the baby, who sniffed and nipped back at him.

'I think you're on to something, Frazer,' she said. 'And it looks to me that he's found a kid sister, as well as a mum.'

Frazer grinned. 'Don't you reckon they're kinda acting like a parent and a teenage kid who's been naughty, but is sorta sorry and wants to get back in his mom's good books?'

'Do you think that they could maybe, er, hang out together?' asked Amazon. 'He could help look after Goldilocks, and the mother could teach him how to do real bear stuff.'

'Can we go now?' said Ben, before Frazer could answer. The little boy was still clinging to Amazon, just as Goldilocks was clinging to her mother. 'I've had enough of the bears.'

Frazer was just thinking of the long trek home – easier, perhaps, without Goldilocks, but still likely to be an ordeal – when he heard a sound that somehow screamed of humanity. And not in a good way.

It was the click of a rifle being cocked.

'You kids stand back out of the way,' came a gruff voice. 'You're safe now. I got them murdering bears right in my sights.'

They spun round to see two men wearing filthy camouflage outfits. They each held a rifle aimed at the bears.

'No!' screamed Amazon. She realized that they were some of the hunters who had come out into the wilderness to shoot any pale-coloured bears. The new family was in mortal danger. 'These bears didn't kill anyone. We've found Ben. He's right here, unharmed.'

'Little lady, you let us decide what to shoot. Now stand aside or –'

The hunter never finished his sentence.

47

Bear Sacrifice

For the first time since his true mother had been lost, the great bear was happy. He knew at some level that these others weren't quite the same as him, but they were close, close enough. He had saved the little one from the trap. And the big one . . . she would look after him. She would show him how to do the things that bears do. How to fish, and find berries, and dig into bees' nests for the honey and the grubs. And he would use his strength and his might to defend them from anything that would try to hurt them.

He did not fear the small humans who had tried to steal the baby away. He was aware that they were still close, but to him they mattered no more than the trees or the rocks.

He had found his family.

Then he heard that click. It was the click that came before the bang that took away his first mother, his true mother. He looked up and saw that there were big humans there, beyond the small ones.

He stood.

These ones would not be permitted to harm his new mother, his baby sister. He would protect them. He would . . . kill.

He got clumsily to his feet, pushing the mother and the baby away from him, away from danger.

And then he charged.

48

The Shot

Amazon had her back to the bears. She was facing the two hunters, trying to stay in between them and their prey. Frazer was doing the same – they both knew that the hunters would never risk firing through them.

Because their backs were to the bears they never saw the charge.

But Ben, who was still clinging to Amazon, looking back over her shoulder, did.

What he saw was a bear apparently charging straight at him.

He screamed.

Amazon and Frazer both turned.

They saw the great pale beast eating up the few metres between them. They both knew instinctively that he was not coming for them. They knew that he was trying to save the family that he had only just found.

Yet still it was the most frightening thing any of them had ever seen.

And then the rifle shot rang out – a sharp but strangely quiet sound, almost like a heavy 'tut' from a cross schoolteacher – and the bear stopped, looking almost surprised. It seemed to gather itself again and began to come on. But its mighty front legs buckled beneath it and it fell, almost comically – had it not, that is, been so tragic – right at their feet.

Amazon spun again to scream at the hunters, or rather at the murderers. She saw that they had already turned to run. One had even dropped his rifle – or hurled it away in terror.

And she saw something else. Standing by the wreckage of the aircraft some twenty metres away was another man. He was also holding a rifle. A very strange-looking rifle.

'Uncle . . .?'

'DAD!'

It was Hal Hunt, looking gaunt and resolute. He was carrying the X-Ark – the high-precision tranquillizer gun favoured by TRACKS.

New Mysteries

A few minutes later, they were gathered together under the wing of the wrecked aircraft, sheltering from the falling snow.

The two scruffy hunters, whose rifles had been confiscated by Hal Hunt, were arguing.

'How could you drop your gun like that? When it went off, it cudda blowed my head off.'

'Well, you started running, an' it sorta spooked me. If you hadn't been yella, I'd have –'

'I suggest,' said Hal in a voice made more intimidating by its quiet precision, 'that you gentlemen shut your mouths and get the heck out of my sight, before I decide to put *you* to sleep, and lay you down next to that bear.' He tapped the X-Ark. 'And, believe me, he'll wake up long before you will.'

The two hunters gulped.

'OK,' said the first hunter, 'but I gotta report in this whole incident, including this here crashed aircraft and those freaky bears.'

'Yep, you should probably do just that,' said Hal Hunt.

'Can we have our guns back?' said the second hunter.

'Sure. You can get them back from the Canadian Mounted Police station in Prince William. That's supposing you have the right permits, of course. The Canadian government is very strict, I understand, on the legality of carrying firearms in the State Parks . . .'

The hunters looked at each other shiftily, and then headed off back into the woods, still arguing.

'Told you we shoulda gotten them permits . . .' was the last thing they heard.

Alone at last, the three Trackers embraced.

Hal's eyes were moist.

'I was worried about you. I thought I might have lost you as well . . . And look at this big boy! Ben, I know a mom and dad who are going to be very pleased to see you.'

'I bet I get a really gigantic present,' said Ben, a broad white smile on his grimy face.

'How did you find us, Dad?' asked Frazer.

'The GPS function on your watches. I could track you on my laptop. Or get a rough fix at least. I flew the plane in and landed on a lake five miles that way.' Hal pointed down the canyon.

Amazon couldn't control herself any longer.

She hadn't wanted to talk about her parents' disappearance in front of the hunters, but now she had to ask.

'This is it, isn't it? This is my mum and dad's plane. Where are they? What's happened?'

Hal nodded. 'We'll talk about that in a moment. But first you tell me your story. How did you come to be out here?'

And now at last Amazon and Frazer, with frequent interjections from young Ben, explained everything that had happened. The radio news announcement that made them realize that Hal was looking in the wrong place for Ben, the bike ride, the cougar, the landslide, the mother and baby bear, the wolves, and finally the discovery of the wrecked plane . . .

'That's some story,' said Hal, shaking his close-cropped, grizzled head. 'You're lucky to be alive.'

'What can we do with the big bear?' asked Amazon. 'Frazer thinks it's a cross between a grizzly and a polar bear. A grolar . . .'

'Yep, I reckon he's right.'

'We think it might have wanted to join the others, as a . . . family.'

The mother and baby bear had run away into the forest at the shot and had not yet returned.

Hal shook his head.

'No, that can't work. They're different species and they just don't belong together.'

'Well, what's going to happen to it?' asked Frazer.

He was worried in case his father was going to say that it would have to be put down.

'What it needs is its own kind. And at the moment that means in a zoo or wildlife park. I know the people at Copenhagen Zoo, where they have a female grolar that was reared there. I'll pull some strings. It'll mean getting a freight-carrying helicopter out here, but that's what TRACKS does. I'll call one up on the sat phone.'

At the thought of the bear and its lost family, Amazon's eyes began to fill with tears.

'Now, Uncle Hal, tell me, this is my parents' plane, so where are they?'

'They were obviously here, and not long ago,' said Hal, surveying the scene. He walked round the site, looking at the discarded rubbish and mess. Then he knelt down in the circle of flattened grass that Amazon had noticed earlier.

'Talking of helicopters, one has already been here, earlier today, unless I'm mistaken,' he said thoughtfully.

Amazon gasped.

'That must be the one we heard this morning!' exclaimed Frazer. 'I knew it wasn't just the thunder.'

'Hey, I heard the hellycopter before *anyone*!' said Ben, who had been listening carefully to everything that was said.

'Sure it was,' said Amazon, and then spun back to face Hal Hunt. 'You mean they were rescued?' Her mind was buzzing with hope and confusion.

Hal slowly shook his head.

'I've been in radio contact with the authorities. They would have let me know. This was something else. It looks to me like they've been *taken*.'

'Taken?' said Frazer. 'What do you mean . . . like kidnapped?'

'Possibly, yes.'

'Why do you think that, Dad?'

'I'll talk you through it. We know that Roger and Ling-Mei had found out something important, something earth-shattering, and they were flying back to tell me about it face to face. Their plane came down, and we heard nothing more. Now look at this crash site: you can see that they've made a real effort to hide the wreck. The branches have been cut and folded over so it's almost invisible from the air.

'Why would they do that? Wouldn't you think they'd want to be rescued? That suggests to me that they knew that someone – the bad guys – were after them. And then there's the evidence of the helicopter landing – a helicopter that the authorities know nothing about. And it's obvious to anyone that the camp was searched. For what, I don't know.'

Frazer looked at Amazon. To his astonishment she was grinning.

'Zonnie,' he said, disturbed. 'What are you laughing at? Did you hear what my dad just said? Your parents may have been kidnapped.'

Amazon's smile became even broader.

'Don't you understand, Frazer? If they've been kidnapped, it means that THEY ARE ALIVE! ALIVE! ALIVE! I'd given up hope. I thought they were dead and gone forever. If someone's kidnapped them, it means that they want to keep them alive for some reason. There's hope. It's all I needed, a tiny ray of hope. We'll find them, Uncle Hal, won't we?'

Hal looked her straight in the eye.

'Yes, Amazon, we'll find them. I don't know how, but yes, we'll find and free your parents, I swear it.'

They had been standing close to the dead fire. Now Hal Hunt began to kick lightly at the ash and cinders, a thoughtful expression on his face.

'What is it, Dad?' Frazer asked.

'Just a hunch. Roger and I used to play spies a lot when we were kids. Hiding secret messages, stuff like that. There was one trick we learned from some dime-store book on being a secret agent. It was full of junk, but it had some good ideas on where to hide your papers, or where to leave things if you wanted your partner to find them.'

'And one of them,' said Frazer, getting excited, 'was underneath a fire!'

Hal didn't answer, but reached down into the cold ash. He pushed aside the soil beneath it and pulled something out.

It was a little leather-bound notebook. The cover was scorched black, but it had not been consumed by the fire, and had partially protected the paper within.

Hal Hunt grunted, and Amazon and Frazer gathered closer. Hal opened the book and began to read. Then he closed it again and handed it to Amazon.

'You should be the first,' he said.

'What is it, Dad?' asked Frazer.

But it was Amazon who answered.

'It . . . it's a diary,' she said. 'The diary of . . . Roger Hunt.'

TOP 10 FACTS: SPIRIT (KERMODE) BEARS

1. **KERMODE 'SPIRIT' BEARS** are a sub-species of the black bear race but about 1/10 have white coats.

2. **SPIRIT BEARS** only live on the Pacific coast of British Columbia in Canada.

3. Scientists estimate there are less than four hundred **SPIRIT BEARS** in that area.

4. **KERMODE BEARS** are sacred to the local Native American culture because of their unique colouring.

5. According to Native American legend, **SPIRIT BEARS** are a reminder of times past, specifically the white colour of ice and snow. The master of the universe created one white bear for every ten black bears as a reminder of the hardships during the Ice Age.

6. **KERMODE BEARS** may have evolved over the last 10,000 years from black bears that became isolated on the coast more than 300,000 years ago.

7. Living in lush forests, **KERMODE BEARS** are lucky to have lots of food – they eat fruits, bulbs, insects, rodents and nuts in addition to salmon.

8. Because of their light fur, **SPIRIT BEARS** are less visible to fish than black bears, making them 30 per cent more efficient at capturing salmon.

9. They can run up to 50 km per hour.

10. **KERMODE BEARS** were named after Francis Kermode, former director of the Royal British Columbia Museum.